Touch

ALSO BY OLAF OLAFSSON

NOVELS

Absolution (1994)

The Journey Home (2000)

Walking into the Night (2003)

Restoration (2012)

One Station Away (2017)

The Sacrament (2019)

SHORT STORIES

Valentines (2007)

Touch

A NOVEL

Olaf Olafsson

ecco

An Imprint of HarperCollins*Publishers*

Many thanks to Lorenza Garcia for her invaluable
assistance when writing this book.

TOUCH. Copyright © 2022 by Double O Investment Corp. All rights re-
served. Printed in Canada. No part of this book may be used or reproduced
in any manner whatsoever without written permission except in the case of
brief quotations embodied in critical articles and reviews. For information,
address HarperCollins Publishers, 195 Broadway, New York, NY 10007.

HarperCollins books may be purchased for educational, business, or
sales promotional use. For information, please email the Special Markets
Department at SPsales@harpercollins.com.

Ecco® and HarperCollins® are trademarks of HarperCollins Publishers.

FIRST EDITION

Designed by Paula Russell Szafranski

Library of Congress Cataloging-in-Publication Data has been applied for.

ISBN 978-0-06-322698-2

22 23 24 25 26   FB   10 9 8 7 6 5 4 3 2 1

Touch

I am going to do my best to leave everything in order when I lock up for the last time. I'm already making good progress, as there is nothing really holding me back. After the staff went home last night, I sat in the office and wrote myself a to-do list which I revised this morning when I got up. I didn't sleep well, was woken by a sudden storm battering the house. Gusts of wind whipped the branches of the ash tree against my bedroom window, creating a strangely rhythmical din I actually found quite comforting. As I lay awake, I used the time to run through the list in my head but stopped short of scrambling out of bed to add to it. That said, I don't believe I had forgotten anything when I returned to it after breakfast.

It feels strange to think that only three weeks ago there were eighty wedding guests here. The groom was Icelandic and the bride Danish, which was reflected in the menu: *stjerneskud* as a starter, rack of lamb for the main. I have catered many wedding parties in my time and can safely say there's nothing I haven't seen. Sometimes I think I glimpse the cracks even before the poor couple have taken their vows; sometimes I feel an overwhelming urge to warn them. Not so with the Icelandic lad and the Danish girl. I have seldom seen two people so in love.

I am going to let this be the last memory of my restaurant. The happy celebrations, and that relaxed, natural affection evident in the young couple's smiles and mannerisms, their thoughtfulness and modesty, the words that didn't need to be said, the deep love they felt for each other which lighted up the room when they walked in. I have been thinking about them this morning. I hope they have avoided the virus and that they are well, wherever they may be. They only need each other.

We stayed open as long as possible, probably longer than we should have. People had largely stopped coming in even before the ban on social gatherings came into effect. We had the odd evening booking, mostly tourists, and when they dried up too, we did our best to keep going by offering deliveries and takeaways—fine food at a fine price, as we advertised on our website. That worked quite well for a few days, but then interest waned, or people became more afraid of getting infected and stopped calling or ordering online. I had managed to buy a consignment of disposable boxes and containers for the food that left the restaurant and am now paying for my optimism, as we have used only a fraction of them. I have just added a reminder to my list to give the rest to the owners of two restaurants in the neighborhood still trying to keep things going. They can do with all the help they can get. For my part, I won't be needing them, as I do not intend to reopen.

There is an echo when I walk across the floor. I pause in the dining area, look around the way I did when I first came here just over twenty years ago. The anticipation I felt then has been replaced by a sense of gratitude. I felt at home the instant I walked through the doors and decided there and then to lease the space. It needed very little work in the way of repairs and refurbishment, as the steakhouse that was here previously never really took off, and closed down after a short time. Admittedly, I bought a better stove, painted the walls in warmer tones, hung some nice pictures, and installed new lighting. But that was it, and we opened only a month after I had signed a six-year lease with Frissi. We have renewed it three times to date, and all I can say about Frissi is that he has been a reasonable and good landlord. In the wake of the financial collapse, he lowered the rent without me even asking. He called me up one Monday morning and said in his hoarse voice: "There's no need for you to go bankrupt. Just pay me half until things improve. In exchange, Bogga and I can eat with you for free when she can't be bothered to cook." Frissi is also on my to-do list, since I intend to settle up with him as with everybody else, preferably by paying him the fourteen months left on the lease.

This is no ordinary echo—any more than the silence brooding over the city. Even standing still, I have the impression I can hear it. But then I pull myself together and clear my throat more forcefully than necessary because I prefer to hear a new echo rather than the one resounding only in my head.

Last night Baldur stood up in the middle of dinner and announced his desire to say a few words. I would have liked it better if he hadn't, but I guess he felt he needed to. Back when I hired him, nearly fourteen years ago, he was a young man of twenty or so, but now he is married with two children. He started as a sous-chef but quickly showed talent and has been running the kitchen for almost ten years. He had handwritten the menu and presented me with it after he finished his speech. "The last supper," he declared, although he hadn't written that on the sheet of paper, "the last supper, Kristófer." There were eight of us at the round table over by the window, the entire staff except for Gunnar and Fjóla, who are in quarantine. Baldur was probably the only sober one among us. I had opened a few bottles of wine I had stored away, some for as long as twenty or thirty years, for we all needed some cheering up. Baldur isn't in the habit of expressing his feelings the way he did that evening, but emotions are running high these days. I did my best to lighten things up, recounting some amusing stories from the past, and I think everybody managed to forget the present, for a while at least.

Today I am going to pay wages and settle bills. Tomorrow I will tidy up. Later in the week I plan to give the place a final scrub. I have already worked out that I can afford to pay the staff until at least the end of September, possibly longer. But today, after I take a closer look at the accounts and the various outstanding bills, I will have a better sense of where I stand. I would like to pay Baldur and Steinunn until the end of the year; they have worked here the longest and genuinely deserve it.

I make myself coffee, turn on the computer, and go over my to-do list. Before making a start, I take a look at the latest news online, most of which is about the progress of the epidemic both here and abroad, but then I decide to quickly check my Facebook page. I find a couple of jokes that actually make me laugh and a few messages I reply to, although none urgent, mostly people responding to our announcement that we are closing, affectionate notes of appreciation. Just as I am about to close the page and turn my attention to the things on my list, I notice a friend request. I receive a lot of friend requests from people I don't know or who perhaps don't even exist, but as always, I open it anyway. And then the name leaps out at me, the decades seem to melt away, and I am standing again in gentle rain outside the locked door, the morning I discovered that they had disappeared.

I am of two minds about whether I should bring my teacup with me. It really doesn't make much sense to be taking up space if I am not checking any bags, which I don't think I should be doing. Besides, I doubt I will have much opportunity to be making my own tea. But I am set in my ways and the cup has become like an extension of my hand, since I use it for coffee as well as tea, though strictly speaking, this is rather against the rules. It's a Japanese earthenware *yunomi* teacup, nothing special, just an everyday-use cup without a handle, most likely from a town called Mashiko, known for its pottery. On it is a tiny picture of a bird perched on a branch, or maybe it's a squirrel. I have never been able to decide which.

I accepted the friend request as soon as I felt the strength return to my hands. Afterward I sat staring at the computer screen for the better part of an hour, motionless, waiting for a reply before realizing it could be a long wait and that in the meantime I ought to be getting on with my tasks. But I had great difficulty concentrating and struggled to work out the salaries and pay the bills; I got in trouble with my online banking, which is unusual for me. Finally I gave up and, instead of banging my head against the wall, used some of the breathing exercises I have recently learned to try to calm myself down.

I asked myself whether the fact that I was holding the teacup when I received her friend request wasn't a clear sign. A sign of something of significance, I mean, something outside what we are capable of putting a finger on, a signal from a guiding force, to put it plainly. But when I came to my senses, I told myself there was nothing remarkable about me sitting at my computer with the cup in my hand; that happened all the time, I should just take a deep breath.

Even so, I was on tenterhooks and decided I should get some fresh air. I called the two restaurant owners, who gratefully accepted the offer of the containers, as they can expect a shortage if their delivery business takes off. I carried the boxed containers out to the car, only half listening to the twelve o'clock news as I drove—that is, until they mentioned flight schedules. "An Icelandair flight to London departed from Keflavík Airport this morning," the announcer declared. "All thirty-one of the airline's other scheduled flights have been canceled." Afterward they went back to talking about infection levels, the numbers of people in intensive care, the shortage of test swabs.

One of the restaurants is on Hverfisgata. The owner, Viktor, came outside to collect the boxes. He is about the same age as Baldur and is also a talented chef. We maintained a two-meter distance. A week ago, we would have commented on this. Now it just seems normal. He said he had heard I was planning to close permanently. I told him it was true. "I'm quitting while I'm ahead," I said, and wished him success.

I will be seventy-five this year. I consider this no age at all, as I am in good health except for a bit of arthritis in my right knee and the occasional arrhythmia which I hardly notice and which my GP tells me is nothing to worry about. It doesn't stop me from hiking in the mountains or doing push-ups on the living room floor at home. I don't consider myself in a high-risk category, but nonetheless I try to behave sensibly, since this virus does not seem to be kind to people my age. It's probably just as well, if worse came to worst, that nobody is dependent on me.

Perhaps I should add: for the time being. I am in good health *for the time being*. And leave it at that, for there is no point in worrying about unconfirmed speculations made by the specialist who I am not at all convinced knows what he is talking about.

The other restaurant is on Laugavegur, just down from the sandwich shop I ran before I opened Torg. I left the boxes by the side door, as the owner wasn't expecting to arrive at work until the afternoon. Before climbing back into the car, I looked up and down the street. It was completely deserted.

When I got back, I sat down at the computer, but there was nothing new. I had checked Facebook on my phone while I was out, but somehow I trust the computer more. It was eleven o'clock in Japan. Nighttime. I told myself I probably wouldn't hear anything until the next day.

I finished paying the salaries and most of the bills, then called the suppliers who had yet to invoice me to ask if they would do so as soon as possible. They all offered me a grace period, assuring me there was no hurry and that I had their backing if I needed. I thanked them for their generosity and support but told them I had made the decision to call it a day. Final decision.

I didn't feel like going home and instead heated up some leftovers for my dinner. I had grown accustomed to the echo, and although I wasn't consciously evoking memories, they inevitably came back to me—mostly happy ones, I must say, for I think everybody, customers and staff alike, generally had a good experience here at Torg.

It was after eight o'clock when I started to think about turning off the lights and heading home. I had done everything I set out to do, just needed to give Frissi a call because I didn't want to transfer money into his account without letting him know first.

I wasn't expecting anything when I checked my Facebook page. I'd been about to switch off the computer and just opened Facebook for the hell of it. But then I saw her reply staring at me. She had written it twenty minutes earlier.

"My name is Miko Nakamura, née Takahashi. Are you the Kristófer Hannesson who lived in London in 1969?"

The pale morning light seeps in through the curtains. As I drowse, I think I can hear the sea, the ebb and flow of distant waves. It's in the morning that I sometimes find it difficult to orient myself, but not today, as I am perfectly aware that I am only imagining the sea's murmur. And yet the sound is pleasant, the steady breathing, so clear I might almost convince myself there is somebody sleeping next to me.

I have decided to take the teacup with me, although to be honest, it's rather impractical. My carry-on bag isn't big and will easily fit in the overhead compartments of both aircraft, as I found out last night when I booked my flights. There is a bit more space on the plane to Japan than on the one to London, between a centimeter and two all around.

It was almost two in the morning when I finally went to bed. We exchanged messages for about half an hour, until she said she needed to rest. By then she had told me about having been hospitalized with the virus. In the next sentence she admitted she wouldn't have tried to find me otherwise. She said it without preamble. Together with a few other things I am still digesting.

I was on the verge of asking if I could call her, but I didn't. And I don't regret it. Knowing her, she would have managed to wriggle out of it.

Knowing her . . . It's a strange thing to say. And yet it hardly felt as if almost half a century has passed since we last saw each other, especially not after we had finished asking the usual polite but trivial questions and provided equally inconsequential answers. She was the one who took the initiative and ended the small talk, as she seemed in a hurry to say what was on her mind.

On the other hand, she was more guarded when I asked how she was feeling.

"A neighbor does the shopping for me," she replied, "she leaves the groceries outside my door. I don't have much of an appetite."

By then I had learned that she lives alone. She and her husband had been childless. "I lost my wife, Inga, seven years ago," I replied. "We had no children either."

She didn't ask me to come. Not even indirectly. And I didn't mention to her I was thinking about it. In fact, it was only later, after we ended our conversation and I was back home contemplating the trees in the garden, that I convinced myself I would never find peace of mind if I didn't go to her.

No sooner had I bought my tickets than a feeling of calm invaded me. Soon afterward the wind that had been blowing all evening dropped as well, and it started to snow. It had been a week of stormy weather, but now big fat snowflakes were floating to the ground like on a pretty Christmas card, settling on the drab lawn and naked branches, covering them so completely that they appeared painted white. I cast my eye over my to-do list, crossed out the tasks I had finished, added some new ones, and then went to bed.

Miko Nakamura . . . née Takahashi. The woman I have never told anybody about. Not my friends or the people I worked with all those years, not my parents or my brother, nobody, not even after I came back from London and they couldn't understand why I was so unhappy. And of course not Inga. Least of all her.

I can see from the light that the snow hasn't melted overnight. The brightness is a sign that the weather has cleared and the sun is beginning to shine. I run over the day's tasks in my mind, decide how best to go about them, and wonder if I have left anything out.

Before I open my eyes completely, I practice the exercises I have been training myself to carry out these past few weeks. I start by remembering my ID card number, then my bank account number, my parents' dates of birth and death, the names of all the Icelandic presidents, some of the newest dishes on our menu, and finally the tasks I added to my to-do list last night before going to bed.

When I am reasonably satisfied with the result, I get up and draw the curtains. The sun is shining on the snow. In the branches of the old spruce, a thrush is singing its lungs out. I have a sense of anticipation in my chest, a burning anticipation that takes me by surprise and reminds me that not so long ago I was a young man.

I could have set off tomorrow morning, but then I worry I wouldn't have time to get everything done, as I am not a fast worker. This is nothing new; I have always needed peace and quiet to do things properly and therefore have learned to avoid rushing. But it also has occurred to me that I may never come back, and this has given me even more to think about. I am not saying this to be dramatic or elicit sympathy, because of course it's very unlikely that I will be prevented from returning. However, nothing is certain these days and I wouldn't wish to leave my affairs in disarray.

Naturally, I mentioned none of this to Mundi when I called him just now. Mundi is my older brother; he lives in a retirement flat in a house for the elderly down by the harbor. I went to see him a week or so ago, but now home visits are no longer permitted.

I had to raise my voice so he could hear me. "Don't you have your hearing aids in?"

"What?"

"Your hearing aids, Mundi. Why haven't you put them in?"

My brother is terribly vain, even when he's alone.

"I don't want to look like an old fart, damn it."

"You're eighty-three, Mundi."

I told him I had booked a flight to Japan.

"About time. You've always talked about going there."

I corrected him and told him it's been years since I last mentioned going to Japan.

"How long are you staying?"

I said I wasn't sure. I had booked my return flight in three weeks' time, but that could change.

"So one of your people will deliver my meals while you're away?"

Mundi has always been a fussy eater and complains to me about the food they provide in the residence, although I don't see a problem with it, it's just standard home cooking. But there is no use arguing with him, and ever since he moved in there, I have humored him by sending him meals as often as three or four times a week. I have been dreading having to tell him those deliveries are now a thing of the past.

"I've closed down, Mundi."

"What?"

"It makes no economic sense to stay open. Anyway, I've had enough."

"You should have seen the fish that idiot served yesterday," he said. "He would have been thrown overboard if he'd dared serve that on my ship."

For over thirty years Mundi was a skipper on one of the big freight ships, and he still treats people as if they are members of his crew.

"How will you fill the time if you close the place?"

I hadn't given it any thought, or rather I had put off thinking about it. "Well, I'm going to start by taking this trip," I said.

"If you think that having nothing to do is desirable, then you're mistaken. If you think you can listen endlessly to the radio or play solitaire, think again. Kristinn, who lived on the floor below, died of boredom the other day. Literally, Kristófer. Fell stone dead in the middle of his living room."

I refused to get excited even if he talked as though I were to blame for his fellow resident's death. He has always been like this, it's just his manner. And yet I wanted to end by saying something meaningful, something he would remember, as I doubted I would be calling him from Asia.

"We've both had good lives," I began, not knowing exactly where I was going with this. In any event he spared me the trouble.

"We're having fish cakes today," he said. "And what do you think they're made of?"

He said goodbye somewhat irritably and again I tried to ignore him. I used to find it hard not to let him upset me, but thankfully this is no longer the case. It's good to know that at least in some respects I have made progress over the years.

Dying alone. Miko said that was her biggest fear. Not death itself but having nobody by her side.

"There's even a word for it," she wrote. *Kodokushi*. And then she added a smiley face—exactly as I would have expected from the girl I knew half a century ago.

I didn't put the funeral on my to-do list. It just felt wrong. Or should I say I was about to, but then I changed my mind before setting pen to paper. "Pay salaries, speak to Sonja, clean stove, go to recycling center, bury Jói Steinsson . . ." No, that would have been inappropriate. Yet I was worried I might forget and considered writing it on a separate piece of paper, but by then I had already made up my mind that I owed it to myself to remember, and so I left it.

The funeral is at two o'clock. The day before yesterday, I called his widow, Aldís, to offer my condolences. She wasn't around when Jói and I were students together in London, and as he and I rarely met after we both returned to Iceland, I hardly know her. I came back first, for I no longer had any reason to stay there after I stopped searching for Miko and Takahashi-san. When Jói finished his studies, he got a job at the National Statistical Institute of Iceland and married soon after.

The few times Jói and I bumped into each other, we got along well enough. We would reminisce about our time in London, especially Jói, who seemed to miss it. "Those were the good old days, Kristófer," he used to say, and I saw no reason to contradict him.

He is being buried at Fríkirkjan, the Lutheran free church in Reykjavík. It's close to my house, walking distance, in fact. As I am putting on my suit, I wonder whether I shouldn't try to fit it in my suitcase. I even go as far as to imagine the circumstances in which I might need it, but I push these thoughts aside and decide to leave it behind. The suitcase isn't big, so I need to choose my clothes wisely and pack them carefully.

I arrive in good time because churches are subject to the ban on social gatherings. Aldís reminded me of this when I called her. "We're expecting more people than there's space for," she said.

The usher guides me to a pew. Every other row is empty, and the funeral-goers are seated two meters apart. People enter one by one to the strains of the organ, Bach and Schubert, also the Beatles—"*Michelle, ma belle*" . . . I can't help thinking of the night when Jói and I got drunk in Piccadilly and he gave me a piggyback ride to Trafalgar Square. Resting on the way, of course, as he sang one Beatles song after the other, including "Michelle," and refused to give up until we got there.

"I'm a man of my word," I remember him saying as we headed down Whitcomb Street, doubtless to spur himself on, because he certainly needed it. The journey seemed endless, especially the last stretch, and I was afraid he might drop me a couple of times when he appeared to stumble. Being drunk took the edge off my anxiety, but I breathed more easily when I finally caught a glimpse of King George IV astride his horse, and together we sang "Michelle," or was it "Norwegian Wood," I don't recall.

He died of cancer, not the virus. Apparently he had been battling it for a few years. The priest uses that word, "battle." He also talks about stoicism, conscientiousness, and integrity, to name but a few of Jói's attributes. He speaks about Jói's family—his wife, Aldís, their daughter and son, their five grandchildren. The terraced house in Fossvogur that it was always such a pleasure to visit, Jói's work for the Iceland Touring Association, his presidency of the Rotary Club, his reliability. The priest mentions the word "contentment" often, it is indeed the mainstay of his tribute, and I can't help wondering if, back when we were students in London, Jói imagined that his life would turn out the way it did. Back then, he had his wild side and was quite ambitious. He played the guitar and liked to defend Ludwig von Mises's theories to our more radical lecturers and Keynesianism to those who embraced unbridled market forces. There was a Swedish professor, for example, who used to get on Jói's nerves, and he didn't hesitate to debate him, even though in those days it wasn't the custom for students to do much talking. But Jói was a star student and got away with things others could not. When he landed the job at the National Statistical Institute, he said he didn't plan on staying there long—only until he had settled down, it was more or less a home for geriatrics, a basic requirement of the people who worked there not to tax their brains too much.

"Forty-five years," the priest says, "content and productive, he made his contribution to society."

I wonder again how Jói envisioned his future back when we were young. And how I envisioned mine. Certainly not the way it turned out. And yet I am content in many ways, in most ways, for as I said before, I have much to be grateful for. Is there any reason for me to suppose that Jói was not?

Instead of asking questions I'll never know the answer to, I remind myself I must contact Sonja sooner rather than later, straight after the funeral, perhaps. I have already written it down on my to-do list and of course I won't forget, and yet something about what the priest was saying makes me think of her and little Villi. Maybe the part about contentment.

They play Albinoni as we leave. I don't recognize the pall-bearers, but I assume they are a mixture of relatives and friends.

The weather has brightened up when I get outside. They have postponed holding a wake until after the pandemic, so I am able to go straight home without offending Aldís and her family.

I pause at Skothúsvegur and watch the light as it breaks through the clouds above Lake Tjörnin. It is still frozen over and seems to lift slightly when the sun shines on it. *"Michelle, ma belle, sont les mots qui vont très bien ensemble, très bien ensemble . . ."* "I'm not giving up, Kristófer, I never give up!" Trafalgar Square looming before us. A slight drizzle. I smile to myself before turning around and continuing up the hill.

Sonja is Inga's daughter from her first marriage. She and her husband, Axel, live in the suburb of Hafnarfjörður, and they have a son, Vilhjálmur Orri—or Villi for short. Sonja was six when Inga and I started living together, and she got used to me rather quickly. We have always gotten along quite well, as it was mostly Inga's role to scold her when necessary. Or so Inga maintained, and I never bothered to argue with her, even though, as I recall, I didn't exactly shirk my duties.

It wasn't long before Sonja started to call me Dad. I never asked her to, although I confess that I was happy about it. I can even remember the first time she did it, so maybe I am not so touched in the head after all. It was a Saturday in the spring; I had gone into the garage to fetch a rake, a trowel, and a few other tools because Inga and I had planned to spend the day gardening. When I heard her yell "Dad" from the house—not once but twice—I assumed her father, Orri, had arrived. I remember being surprised because I didn't know we were expecting him, which was why I walked out to the driveway to greet him. Of course, he wasn't there, and when I glanced at the house and saw Sonja standing in the door looking at me, I finally realized. My heart leaped.

"Dad, will you pump up my bike for me?"

Occasionally I have wondered whether she had already decided to call me Dad before reaching the door or if it happened spontaneously. Not that it matters, but even so I have tried to picture her standing in the doorway looking at me. I have never managed to figure it out either way, but I am inclined to think it came out naturally because she appeared impatient, as if she couldn't believe how long it was taking me to answer her.

She called Orri Dad too. This didn't bother me in the slightest, and as far as I know, he felt the same way. Obviously Orri could have paid more attention to his daughter, but he found it difficult after he remarried and he and his new wife, Eva, started having kids. Inga didn't like Eva, who was without question bossy and maybe a bit selfish as well, which is quite typical in these types of situations. Inga, who was not on the best terms with Orri, tried a few times to speak to him about it but to no avail. On the other hand, Orri and I got along fairly well, which is why in the end Inga asked me to have a word with him. He was frank with me, said he was between a rock and a hard place, and asked if I could help. "Things will get better," he said, "but until they do, I'd be grateful if you could be there for Sonja, more than you are already, and calm Inga down when she's about to fly off the handle."

I honored his request, and why wouldn't I? Perhaps, if I am honest, I liked the idea of having less competition. Not to say that I felt he and I were competing for Sonja's attention, exactly, although afterward I couldn't help thinking that my response may not have been motivated solely by kindness and concern. But that was much later on, after Inga passed away, and it's unnecessary now to be rehashing those speculations.

These experiences proved useful a year or so ago when Gunnar and his partner found themselves in a predicament. What I can say about Gunnar is that he has worked for me for almost ten years, becoming headwaiter in 2016, and is excellent at his job, one of the best in the business, in fact. Gunnar is gay, and rightly I should have referred to his "husband" just now, not his "partner," as they were married last year. Anyway, I noticed he hadn't been himself lately, seemed withdrawn and preoccupied, so I asked him what the matter was. At first he played it down, but then he confided in me that he and his husband (I think his name is Svanur, but I wouldn't swear to it) wanted children and had found a surrogate mother they both thought was perfect. Two children, to be exact; they had agreed that Gunnar would father one and his husband the other. It all seemed terribly well organized to me, but I repressed the urge to tease him about it, even affectionately. Obviously they should have been delighted about finding the perfect surrogate, but instead they had fallen out, and Gunnar didn't know what to do about it. His husband had come up with the idea that the children should call him Dad and Gunnar simply Gunnar. He had announced this as if nothing could be more self-evident, the way someone might discuss what to have for dinner or where to go on summer holiday, and he wasn't expecting Gunnar to protest. Like all good waiters, Gunnar is resourceful and adaptable; he seldom allows any situation to throw him. However, on this occasion he was deeply hurt. He said as much and asked why it couldn't be the other way around, the children could call *him* Dad and his husband by his first name, which, by the way, I am almost certain is Svanur.

They quarreled, and both said things they regretted. Tempers were frayed, but gradually they calmed down, apologized to each other, and agreed they should try to find a sensible solution. And yet despite their good intentions, that approach hadn't

worked. Gunnar told me they had considered several possibili-
ties. One was that the first child should call him Dad and his
partner Svanur, and the second should call Svanur Dad and
Gunnar by his first name. But they realized this would be far
too confusing for the children and even the parents themselves.
Consequently, they resolved to put off having children for a
while and planned to inform the surrogate, at the risk of losing
her to another couple.

I was happy to be able to help them out. It was simple, I said
to Gunnar, the children could call them both Dad, and I explained my own experience with this, which had worked well. Of
course, he asked me a lot of questions, which I had no problem
answering. I also suggested that, if necessary, the children could
call them Daddy Gunnar and Daddy Svanur, which Sonja sometimes did to avoid misunderstandings.

They followed my advice and Svanur even called to thank
me. He took the opportunity to ask me a few additional questions regarding this arrangement, wanting to hear about my experience firsthand, although he insisted that Gunnar had relayed
our conversation to him in detail.

They have a little girl now by the name of Birta, and the
last I knew, they were thinking about having more children. But
that was right before the pandemic, so it wouldn't surprise me
if they changed their minds or at least put these plans on hold.
They have been in quarantine for just over a week now, as one of
Svanur's colleagues tested positive for the virus, although none
of them has symptoms. I plan to call Gunnar today to see how
they are doing, because I haven't heard from him in a couple of
days, and to tell him I have deposited his salary into his account.

Birta has just had her first birthday, so it's still too early for
them to put my advice to the test. I have wondered whether I
wasn't maybe too categorical about it and perhaps didn't prepare
them adequately for the things that can go wrong. But in the

end I don't think there is any need to worry. They make a good team and have the advantage that Birta will become habituated to the arrangement from the very beginning.

I absolutely must call Sonja. For some reason I have been putting it off. I will do it as soon as I have taken this suit off and hung it in the wardrobe. I have made a final decision not to take it with me to Japan.

I was surprised when Sonja decided to write her mother's obituary. Call me old-fashioned, but in my day it wasn't the custom for children to be writing about their parents. Grieving in silence, not on the street—or on the pages of local newspapers—was considered appropriate. But as I say, I expect I am simply out of step with the times.

I was no less taken aback by the content of the obituary, as I had the impression Sonja was writing about a woman I didn't know. Or, to put it bluntly, that she had decided to release her inner storyteller, which I wasn't aware existed.

"Mom always dreamed of living in Hveragerði" was one of the things she wrote. Hveragerði, what nonsense! Inga never said any such thing, not once. She showed no interest whatsoever in the village of Hveragerði, not even back when people first started to flock there on weekends to buy ice cream and cucumbers, to see the monkey on display in one of the geothermal greenhouses. Inga wouldn't even move out of our terraced house in Reykjavík after it became just the two of us, even if it was the most sensible thing to do, as we didn't need two hundred and fifty square meters, not to mention the impending costly renovations I would have gladly done without. But Inga was stuck in her ways, and I decided to do as she wanted and put the subject aside. Just when I was about to raise it again, she fell ill. After that, naturally, it never occurred to me to mention moving.

It would have been wisest for me to ignore the obituary and not to be upset that I found out about it only when I opened the newspaper the morning of the funeral. That would have been by far the wisest thing to do, but I just couldn't help myself. Having decided not to keep quiet, I should have spoken to her face-to-face instead of calling her, but sometimes we don't see these things clearly. I admit I was stupefied. Yes, quite shocked, to be honest.

"Hveragerði?" I said. "Your mother never said a word to me about Hveragerði. Never."

"Maybe not to you. Or maybe you just weren't listening."

"Are you telling me that she spoke to you about wanting to move to Hveragerði?"

"I find it strange that this is what you most noticed in my little piece about Mom," she said.

I didn't respond immediately, because there were other things in the obituary that struck me as odd, but I realized they required a lengthier discussion.

"I noticed a lot of things," I said at last, "misunderstandings I could have put right if you'd shown it to me first. Hveragerði is just one example. I'm sorry you chose to remember your mother in that way."

It might have been tempting to attribute Sonja's strange behavior to the grieving process, though I am never quite sure in which order the five—or is it seven?—stages are supposed to appear. But there was something deeper at work here, something from the past I had evidently missed. Admittedly Inga once said that my indulgence toward Sonja could be interpreted as indifference, but I didn't take her seriously because she was usually in a bad mood when she said things like that.

I always intended to talk more about the obituary with Sonja, but nothing ever came of it. My anger ran its course, if you can call it that, because more than anything, I felt shocked and hurt. I hesitate as well to use the word "hurt," because frankly I was a bit ashamed of having let her upset me to such an extent that I suddenly saw my life with Inga in a different light. A strange light. Distorted and alien, dare I say.

Thankfully these feelings soon passed. I put aside the newspaper and looked at it again only a few days later, didn't read till then the obituaries written by other people, which obviously struck a completely different note than Sonja's. They all portrayed Inga, and our relationship, in a way that did justice to her. By then I had realized that the things that bothered me would doubtless be lost on the general reader, which was precisely the intention. I have to hand it to Sonja, she's not a bad writer and is quite skillful at making oblique remarks.

We sat next to each other in the church. Villi wasn't born yet, but she and Axel had been living together for a few months, and he sat with us. When it was all over, I put my arms around her, and our embrace was prolonged and heartfelt. All the more reason why I was so taken aback when later she criticized me for not crying.

I have again been dragging my feet about calling Sonja, or should I say postponing it. I am not trying to avoid talking to her before I leave and have no intention of putting it off until it's too late; I simply have had other more pressing things on my to-do list. I got in touch with Frissi about the rent, for example, and explained where things stand. As I might have expected, he protested and tried to talk me out of closing, then refused to accept any more rent from me. Finally we agreed I would pay him six months as opposed to the fourteen remaining on the lease. I told him this meant I could give my staff more severance pay and thanked him.

"Where will I go to eat now when Bogga can't be bothered to cook?" he said.

The truth is, he and his wife seldom took advantage of the arrangement we made, and on the rare occasions when they did eat at my restaurant, Frissi insisted on paying for their meal. We succeeded in giving them the odd complimentary appetizer, a glass of wine or dessert, that was all.

"Bogga takes good care of you," I said. "You won't starve."

"She drags me out for a walk twice a day. As if I were a dog. This really is a wretched situation."

I told him I was going abroad.

"What?" he said.

"I'm leaving everything in order so that as of tomorrow you can start showing the space to people," I said. "If you don't mind, I'll see about the furniture when I get back . . ."

He made another stab at talking me out of closing the restaurant but then gave in, said again how awful the situation was and how Bogga was killing him with these endless strolls.

I have finished packing. I wrapped the teacup in plastic and then in a tea towel, although I probably didn't need to. I am taking plenty of socks, underwear, shirts, and T-shirts, as I have no idea when I might be able to do laundry. I am also packing two pairs of trousers and two thin sweaters, as the forecast for the coming days is warm, sixteen or seventeen degrees. And intermittent rain. Which is why I am going to wear my blue windbreaker. It is light and comfortable.

I empty out a bottle of vanilla essence and fill it with aftershave. It's only thirty milliliters and therefore complies with regulations. It should last until I get to Japan, where I plan to buy a proper bottle of cologne. I am taking two books with me: *Japanese for Beginners* and *Traditional Japanese Poetry: An Anthology*, which I bought years ago at Eymundssons in Austurstræti when the collection of traditional haiku that Takahashi-san gave me suddenly vanished from the house. They are both paperbacks and don't take up much room.

I reheat some leftovers again for dinner. After cleaning up, I finally call Sonja.

She doesn't answer and I don't leave a voicemail, there is no point, she will see that I have called. Actually, to be honest, I am relieved and tell myself it's possible she won't call back until tomorrow. Sonja is a geriatric social worker and has had a lot to do since the virus struck. She calls herself a frontline worker. Obviously I don't dispute that, although Sonja likes the limelight and has always been a bit dramatic. She works hard and takes good care of her clients, so I can understand if she is busy.

When Sonja started having regular contact with me again, about two or three years ago, it seems she decided it was best to treat me as if I were one of her clients. Our conversations often consist of her asking me questions and me giving her answers that frequently prompt more questions or the same ones rephrased. For example:

"Do you exercise enough?"

"I think so."

"How many times a week?"

"How many times?"

"Yes, I mean, how often do you go for a walk, for example?"

"I don't really count."

"Would you say twice or . . . ?"

And so it continues, because we are capable of having conversations where all she does is ask questions which I answer, often evasively, as I automatically go on the defensive, needlessly, of course. Her training also seems to have taught her how to ask questions so that they don't come across as criticism but, rather, as solicitation of my opinion. For example: "Do you feel you take enough exercise?" Or "If you had more time, do you think you'd go out for more walks?"

Sometimes I feel like saying I hope for her sake her clients don't find her so transparent, but I restrain myself.

I have been considering driving to Keflavík Airport and leaving the car in long-term parking, but just now while I was eating and thinking about Sonja, I realized this is impractical. First of all, I have no idea how long I will be away, and second, if anything happened to me, I don't want her to have to go to Keflavík to fetch my car. I can see her complaining about the hassle it would involve, hear her voice clear as day, and just thinking about it makes me feel almost guilty. Which is why I decide to leave the car at home and instead take the six a.m. shuttle from the central bus station.

On the box of chocolates is a picture of a mountain which, surprisingly, I do not recognize. The high slopes are dusted with snow, and above them float two fair-weather clouds you might think were always there. Tiny wisps, white as the snow yet broken up in places as if they are just forming or maybe beginning to evaporate. At the foot of the mountain, a stream runs over rocky moorland, slowly, it seems. The sun is high in the sky. It is late spring or early summer.

Nowhere on the box does it say where the photograph was taken, and I am of two minds because I know I will feel a bit awkward if I can't tell her anything about the mountain, should she ask. There are two other boxes, one with a picture of Gullfoss Falls, the other of Geysir, but the first is too big and the second rather small. And although I certainly have no objection to those two marvels of nature, I'm tempted to pick the unknown mountain.

I am alone in the duty-free shop, as the airport is practically deserted. There were only three of us on the bus, and when I walked over to the check-in, the rattle of my wheeled suitcase sounded almost deafening. Here upstairs it's even emptier, so all of a sudden I find myself feeling a bit lonely.

When my phone rings, I jump and the sales assistant seems to as well, although I am standing at least two meters away from her. I get a bit flustered, and it takes me a while to locate my phone in my pocket.

At last I dig it out and ask Sonja to wait a moment while I pay for the box of chocolates and move away from the counter.

"Where on earth are you?"

I tell her.

"What?" she says.

"I called you yesterday to let you know I'm going abroad."

"What do you mean?"

"I'm on my way to Japan."

A silence at the other end merges with the silence surrounding me.

"Japan?" she says at last.

"Yes," I say. "I'm changing planes in London . . ."

"Kristófer . . . Dad, is everything okay?"

"Of course," I say.

"May I ask why you're going to Japan? Now, in the midst of a pandemic?"

"I'm going to visit some friends of mine who live over there," I say.

"Friends?"

I understand that she is taken aback, but I don't see the need for her to carry on in the same astonished tone of voice.

"I've closed the restaurant," I say, and before she asks, I add: "For good."

I don't tell her this to shock her, that isn't my intention, I just want to lay all my cards on the table so she won't be able to accuse me of hiding anything from her.

"Dad," she says, "Dad . . . Shouldn't we . . . Have you checked in yet?"

"Yes, I was buying something in the shop upstairs when you called. I have to go to the departure gate now. My flight is leaving soon."

"Dad, is this really a good idea? . . . Villi was asking after you . . . He wanted to know if you had bought a teddy bear . . ."

I am puzzled, and she explains that during Covid, people have started putting dolls in their windows to amuse the children when they go out for a walk with their parents.

"Villi was hoping to see a teddy bear in your window . . ."

"If only I had known," I say. "It's too late now."

I don't mean to accuse her, but she goes on the defensive.

"How were we to know that you were rushing off abroad . . ."

"My flight is leaving soon," I repeat. "I'll let you know when I arrive."

"Can't we talk about this?"

"Don't worry," I say.

"To be honest, I just don't understand you," she says, forgetting to express her thoughts in the form of questions, which admittedly wouldn't be so easy in this case.

I say goodbye to her, send my love to Villi, but forget to mention Axel. Before I hang up and put my phone back in my pocket, I assure her I will be in touch during my trip, maybe even as soon as London.

I put on my glasses after we disembark and open Facebook on my phone. I haven't heard from Miko since yesterday morning and I am starting to get worried. Hopefully for no good reason, as I remember it took her a while to respond after she first got in touch. I can scarcely believe that was only three days ago.

The plane is half empty. During the flight, I read the newspapers and then take out my notebook and continue my reminiscing. I packed it alongside the book of poems and the language primer; it's the one I kept in my desk at the restaurant. The other three are at home. I prefer this one, not just because it's the easiest to carry around but also because it contains more haikus than the others, both the ones I composed and some by Takahashi-san which I wrote down and which are much better than mine, of course. Although I have to say that the more we sparred with each other, the more accomplished I got. In fact, I remember him saying so.

Haiku is a type of verse made up of three lines consisting of five syllables, seven syllables, and five syllables respectively, and as you might imagine, the trick consists of conveying a thought or a feeling in only a few words yet in a memorable way, to quote Takahashi-san himself. He didn't need to add that this is easier said than done. Actually I remember the first evening we spoke about the trick of writing a good haiku and I asked what it entailed. He said it was simply a question of finding the right words and arranging them in the right order, and then he laughed heartily. He had a habit of joking around and avoiding serious philosophical conversations, and it was easy to see where Miko got her humor from.

The truth is that anyone attempting a haiku, even a novice, has to show some level of ingenuity and be interested in language. Those with more practice learn to fuse words and form so that the haiku in its simplicity and sincerity penetrates the reader's mind and makes them pause, even if only fleetingly. The few who are possessed of genius succeed in seamlessly marrying in these three lines everyday life and the natural cycle, creating a unified image which they then disperse, almost soundlessly, so that the reader cannot help but gasp in awe.

A few years ago, I started to organize some of the haikus Takahashi-san and I composed, the more substantive ones, and wrote them down in this half-empty notebook. Takahashi-san's English wasn't bad, though he insisted his haikus were better in Japanese. Admittedly, Miko had to help him sometimes, mainly with his grammar, and he probably wasn't exaggerating when he claimed it took him much longer to compose in English than in Japanese. And yet none of this showed in his poems, which without exception possessed a sort of wondrousness, albeit a discreet one.

Darkness comes early.
Beneath the flickering stars
streetlamps illumine.

I remember he wrote this in July. I also remember Miko opened the door just as I was taking it out of the pot. It was as if she had brought with her the light he had written about in his poem.

Anyway, as I was saying, she hasn't replied to my last message, which perhaps isn't so strange, as nothing I said required a response. I was mostly thinking and reflecting, contemplating how strange life is sometimes, how relative time can be, that kind of thing. She had just let me have her address; this was the day before yesterday.

"But don't send me anything," she said. "There really is no need."

She has no idea I am on my way to her. I haven't told her yet, and I don't intend to until I am farther along on my journey. Because something can always go wrong, and I don't wish to upset her unnecessarily.

The flight to Tokyo has been delayed until tomorrow. At the check-in desk, two uniformed airline attendants explain to those of us gathered that, owing to the current situation, there is no flight today. However, they say we have all been booked on tomorrow's flight and, when asked, assure us there will be plenty of available seats, so we needn't worry.

It would be more precise to say that today's flight has been canceled, not delayed, but I resist the urge to split hairs, as they are nice people, doing all they can to help. They even offer us a discount at one of the airport hotels, which I think some of my fellow passengers are going to accept. For my part, I have never liked sleeping in those kinds of places; in fact, I avoid them ever since I came down with a stomach bug and was stuck at Heathrow for nearly forty-eight hours. That was ages ago, yet I have never forgotten it—the bleak room, the unpleasant-tasting tap water, the view over the parking lots and warehouses, the peculiar feeling of emptiness that invaded me and drained my energy, even more than the bug itself, and stayed with me longer.

And so, before I know it, I am on the express train heading into central London. I take care to keep my distance from the other passengers, which is easy because the carriage is half empty. Despite having lived here once and even briefly considered settling in the city, now I feel the same as any other tourist, I imagine, a visitor who previously left behind no trace.

I came to London to study economics. There were two Icelanders at the university, Jói Steinsson and I. We got to know each other practically our first day, although neither of us knew about the other beforehand. We soon became friends and study partners and would often meet outside class, especially on weekends, when we could set aside our books and enjoy a beer together. I was fascinated by my studies in my first year; our lecturers were excellent, as were the facilities—the library, for example, couldn't have been better. The university was still relatively peaceful back then; the student protests wouldn't start until my second year, and only in my third year did the uprisings take place. By then everything had changed, including me.

Back when Sonja was still in grammar school, she found an envelope containing photographs from my student days. Some were of me, others of various locations in the city, there were one or two of Jói Steinsson. It was just a random collection of photos I had stuck in an envelope, as one does. They weren't supposed to tell a story, and I didn't think of them as a testament to anything in particular.

What most interested Sonja was how different I looked. She barely glanced at what I considered the most interesting pictures, for example one of the Thames just after daybreak, or Hyde Park in the late afternoon, when the shadows of the trees seemed to take on a life of their own. It was a trick of the light, I told her. But she didn't seem interested and picked out the photographs of me from the pile, returning the others to the envelope.

I had bought myself a Canon camera soon after I arrived in London, and I used it quite a bit, especially during the first few months. The photograph of me outside the entrance to the Old Building was taken by Jói our first week there, and Sonja compared it with another one of me in my last month at the university—just before I quit my studies, to be precise. In the earlier photo I have short hair and am clean-shaven, dressed in gray trousers, a white shirt and a tie, and a tweed jacket I remember buying at a shop on Oxford Street. In the later one my hair is long, I have a beard and am wearing round glasses, the tie has long disappeared, and my jacket looks rather crumpled. I don't remember who took that photograph, but I don't think it was Jói.

Sonja demanded explanations, so I did my best to describe to her what was taking place in the world at the time, about the Vietnam War and its ramifications, the student revolt in France in the spring of 1968, and our activism in London a year or so later. "Did you take part?" she kept asking when I told her about the protests and our conflicts with the university authorities, our bid to occupy part of campus, and how they responded by barricading the entrance as well as the inside of some of the buildings.

"But we managed to break through," I said. "As a result, the university closed down for a whole month. By the time it reopened, I had lost all interest in continuing my studies."

She looked at me and then at the photograph of me with a beard and round glasses as if she couldn't quite believe I was the same man. "You're unrecognizable," she said.

I also let it slip that I had written an article, "Reimagining Socialism," which attracted some attention and became a sort of manifesto for us revolutionaries. What I didn't mention was that Jói Steinsson had renamed it "Reimagining Kristófer" and joked about it with our mutual acquaintances.

I think Sonja felt a tinge of admiration for me and my youthful activism, and I don't mind admitting this made me happy. I don't remember why she had been seeing more of her father around this time, her biological father, that is, but it had affected me more than I had expected.

"Who's this?" she asked, pulling out a photo of Jói and me taken just before Christmas in '68, about a month before the uprising. I told her about my friend.

"He hasn't changed his appearance at all," she said. "He's dressed exactly like you were in the first photo."

"Jói still dresses exactly like I did in the first photo," I remember replying.

Maybe I meant to say more about Jói Steinsson, but I didn't. Sonja wasn't interested in him, anyway; it was my past she was curious about.

"What did you do after you quit university?"

Her question echoes in my head as we pull into Paddington Station. My plan was to search on my phone for a hotel room on the way, but I haven't gotten around to it. I have plenty of time, however, as nothing awaits me except an idle afternoon.

I have installed myself in a cozy room in a small hotel on Monmouth Street. The window overlooks the cobbled street, and if I lean my head out just a bit, I can see the entire row of houses opposite. They are low-rise buildings comprising two or three stories, shops and restaurants at ground level—a café, a newsagent, and a shoe repair shop—offices and flats on the upper floors. There are few people around. It is just after three o'clock.

Needless to say, I had plenty of hotels to choose from, and the half-price discount I got here wasn't an exception. This neighborhood wasn't the obvious choice, as it took me nearly an hour to walk here. But my mind was probably taken up with the past, or at least with some leftover memories from when I lived here still floating around in my head, as I barely looked at any other parts of town when I sat down with my phone on a bench outside the station.

But I don't regret it. The hotel is first-rate, and although the room is under the eaves, it is spacious and comfortable. There are some flowers in a vase on a little table in the corner and a bowl of fruit on one of the nightstands. On the shelves are photographs from the old days when the French Hospital was here, as well as a few hardcover books which I haven't had a proper look at yet.

I haven't really thought about walking to the university campus, which is only a short distance away. According to the gentleman in reception, schools might be closing as early as tomorrow, and it is rumored that London will be in lockdown soon. He thought he ought to let me know, although he emphasized that nothing is certain.

"Because in that case we would have to close the hotel," he explained.

On my way here, I came to the realization that now is a good time for me to confront a few things I haven't given much thought to in recent years or perhaps have avoided thinking about. Not so much because I have anything to feel ashamed of but because dwelling on the past can be time-consuming and unproductive. But now, all of a sudden, my time is my own and I have nothing better to do, not today, in any case. What my doctor said also comes back to me, about how many people in my situation, in addition to doing the exercises he has given me, find it rewarding and liberating to tackle unresolved issues from their past. I told him I didn't carry around that kind of baggage, and I wasn't aware of any issues I needed to resolve, that maybe I was lucky that way. Then he backed off and talked instead about the need to tie up loose ends, or words to that effect.

It was recalling my conversation with Sonja about the photographs that got me reflecting about the past. Admittedly, I had already started thinking about my student days at Jói's funeral, because the priest did say a few words about his time at LSE and even talked about volume and price indexes, income approaches and national accounts. It's only natural that he felt obliged to say something about Jói's studies and work, but he was clearly on shaky ground, as one might have expected. More than once did he stumble over a word or a phrase, particularly when he decided to mention specific terms or concepts; he undoubtedly would have done himself a favor by sticking to more general themes. He looked noticeably relieved when he was able to resume talking about contentment and happiness.

Anyway, as I was saying, I had just gotten up from the bench outside Paddington Station and decided to walk to the hotel when I started to think again about my student days here in London and my discussion with Sonja about them. As we sat at the coffee table with those old photographs, I explained to her that I had lost interest in economics and started to question its relevance in a world I felt needed a radical rethink, an overhaul, even. I remember this was the gist of what I said, maybe not word for word, but I certainly made a direct connection between my quitting university and what was happening in the world at large at the time. Sonja was curious, as I said before; she hung on my every word and seemed to have discovered a new side to me—or even another, more interesting person. Following our conversation, she started to find out more about that era, even dug up my old Beatles records and played them in the living room, where I still had a gramophone. Her attitude changed; she seemed to have more respect for me.

As is often the case, the truth was a little more complicated than the version I wanted to present to Sonja. Not that I was deceiving her, but I probably could have been a bit more explicit.

The truth is, I was a good student in grammar school, my grades attest to that. I also did a lot of extracurricular reading, fiction and nonfiction, and gained a reputation for being a bit of a walking encyclopedia. It made me feel quite important, as people were impressed by my knowledge of the most unlikely topics. Friends and fellow students often came to me when they were stuck for an answer: "I'm sure Kristófer knows," they would say. I won't pretend it displeased me.

I became interested in economics quite by chance when a young man who had just come back from studying in Germany stood in for my history teacher for a few weeks. He was passionate the way young people are when they have new ideas to communicate, and it rubbed off on me. I saw beauty in a subject that most people find dull, admiring how some of the economists we learned about attempted to explain human behavior with precision and accuracy, through numbers, models, and equations. It was probably the concreteness that fascinated me, the definitive relationship between cause and effect.

I worked on a fishing boat in the summer, saved up some money, took out a student loan. When I was offered a place at the London School of Economics, I couldn't have been happier.

I believe it's right to mention that I did well at my studies. Obviously I had to work hard, as did most of my fellow students. Except for Jói Steinsson. He excelled in every subject effortlessly, it seemed.

At first I thought he was simply showing off. I suspected him of studying when we weren't looking—at night, for example, when everybody else was asleep. But my theory came unstuck after we became closer and I could see for myself the way his mind worked.

Even then I assumed his brilliance was confined to subjects requiring a facility for math and numbers, as he was extremely fast at solving any problem he was presented with. What might take me an hour, he finished in ten minutes. He never ceased to be amazed when he saw me puzzling over a question and couldn't refrain from showing me the answer, insisting it was obvious. When I asked him not to, he was taken aback and didn't understand my irritation.

Gradually I came to realize that Jói was as good at writing essays as he was at solving math problems. This became clear in our third term, when we were due to hand in our final essays in macroeconomics. I remember the weather that Friday as I sat down to write, I remember slaving all weekend in the library, I even remember the desk where I sat; somebody had carved the words "Kiss me Sally" on it. I was seeing less of Jói outside class by that time. I wasn't exactly trying to avoid him, but I had started socializing with a different set of people, students he didn't know, so I had less to do with him than previously. But since we were both studying macroeconomics, it was only natural that we compared notes during lunch break that Friday when we were given the essay topics.

Jói usually worked in his room at the dormitory, so I was surprised when he showed up at the library late on Saturday and asked if I wanted to go to the pub that evening. A band he liked was playing. It never occurred to me that he had already finished his essay, and I told him quite simply that I didn't have time to loaf about, as he should understand.

"What? Haven't you finished yet?" he replied.

I am not saying Jói is the reason why I lost interest in my studies. He couldn't help being more talented. He could have been more modest about it, but even so, I am not blaming him.

Naturally I didn't mention Jói Steinsson to Sonja. In fact, I don't think I have ever mentioned him to anyone. Not the part he played in my reassessing my own abilities. Not even to myself, really, if I am honest.

While Sonja and I perused the photographs and talked about my last weeks at the university, the Vietnam War, and the changes it brought, I took the opportunity to impress upon her the importance of trying to find her own path in life. I had never regretted giving up economics, I told her, it had been the right move for me. I adopted a more fatherly tone than usual and had the impression she listened. I think I even succeeded in convincing myself that I had been guided by my ideals at the time, and when at last we stood up from the table, I had a sense that we'd had a meaningful conversation.

"They're fragmented images which I have difficulty piecing together. And bits of sentences that seem to be taken out of context."

"Is this when you're waking up?"

"Yes, normally."

"Normally?"

"Well, nearly always, if you prefer."

"In the mornings?"

"Yes. I don't sleep during the day."

"No, of course not. And apart from that . . . ?"

"Sometimes I feel it takes me a long time to wake up. Longer than before."

"Do you feel disoriented?"

"Well, it's these fragmented images and half sentences . . ."

The doctor has a pleasant manner and always speaks in the same tone, with a soft voice. I am sure he means well, and yet it is a bit like talking to Sonja, because he repeats the same questions over and over, with the requisite subtle nuances. I didn't really notice this until my second visit, when he took me through the test. Then I became aware of the similarities with Sonja and also the differences. Sonja asks questions as if she is trying to extract information from me, whereas the doctor was testing my memory, checking for any discrepancies in my account of things, or so I imagined. The moment I realized this, it occurred to me to tell him I had seen through his technique, as I thought he would give me credit for noticing.

"You're asking the same questions, but you change the words to make it less obvious," I said.

I instantly saw from his reaction that I had made a mistake. He looked a little taken aback, though he tried not to let it show, and then quickly collected himself and asked if this "irritated" me.

Those were his exact words—did this irritate me. Not did it bother me, did I object to it, did it make me feel uncomfortable. Maybe this proves how vague his diagnosis is, possibly even incorrect, seeing as I instantly recalled that very word from the pamphlet my GP gave me before he referred me to this specialist. There it stated quite clearly that people suffering from this disease may get irritated over trivial things. I remembered it because I have always found the word "irritate" rather unattractive. It occurred to me the doctor was testing me again, trying to see if I was showing symptoms that would support his opinion.

"No," I said, "not at all. I only mentioned it because I thought you were checking whether I had noticed."

I don't know why I am thinking about this now. I allowed myself a quick lie-down, as I got up early to leave for the airport, and besides had a somewhat restless night. Otherwise, I wouldn't be sleeping during the day—I was telling the doctor the truth. And I wouldn't say I slept, I simply dozed with one eye open and was aware of myself the whole time, certainly did not have to piece together any fragmented images when I came to.

I had opened the window onto the street. The breeze is quite warm, it's about twelve degrees and overcast, as it often is here in London. I feel a bit tired and don't hurry to get up, and anyway, I am still reflecting about the doctor and our conversation.

He asked about my home life. When I told him I lived alone, he wanted to know who my next of kin was. I said Sonja, of course, and he went on to ask for her phone number, assuring me this was normal practice. "A precaution," he said. "In case anything happens."

But I haven't told Sonja about my visits to the GP or the specialist, and I don't intend to until it becomes necessary. I told him this, explained I didn't think that the time had come. It was evident he wanted me to provide this information, as he was filling out some sort of form on his desk which undoubtedly had a box for Sonja's phone and email and possibly for other relatives if required. He paused, adjusting his glasses with one hand and with the other raising his pen from the paper, clearly unhappy about leaving those boxes empty, because that is the sort of person he is. Which is exactly why I teased him a little when he said something about me living alone. It was harmless but probably unnecessary. "Do you have somebody in mind for me to live with?" I asked. He looked slightly embarrassed, and I quickly added: "I'm just pulling your leg."

He said nothing but nodded, barely smiling.

Now I am wondering if he concluded that I was trying to prove something to him or being defensive, perhaps. Whether, in other words, I was attempting to show him there was nothing wrong with me, that my brain was working perfectly well since I was fully capable of setting him straight if I so chose. I hope not, as it goes without saying that my remark was completely innocent. Even so, I can't help wondering about it as I watch the curtains move in the breeze, because there was no mistaking that he became rather serious after this.

Maybe that's why I decided to lighten the atmosphere a little before the session ended. Following on from his question about whether I always knew where I was when I woke up, to which I had answered yes, I related a recent dream that had stayed with me for several days.

I was at a gathering. There were only men present, all dressed alike. All in dark suits with a white shirt and tie. I could see only myself when I looked down. Then I noticed I was wearing brightly colored socks. Apart from that, I assumed I was dressed the same as the others. Although of course I didn't know for sure. I just felt that I didn't stand out. Anyway, I soon realized about half the guests were deceased. This became clear when we sat down at three long tables, because then it was decided that those who had passed away would sit on the north side while the others sat on the south. This was how it was phrased, I remember that well. The north side and the south side. I'm not sure why that idea was abandoned, but suddenly everybody stood up again, and the people who had passed away could choose where they sat. What I found strangest, I told the doctor, and this was probably why the dream had stayed with me, was that after this switch, there was no way of telling who was dead and who was alive. No way at all.

With this I laughed and expected him to laugh with me, since the aim of my story had been simply to clear the air between us. It's possible he smiled briefly, but then he leaned back in his chair and asked: "Were you on the north side or the south side?"

I smiled, but then it dawned on me that I had no idea. Try as I might, I couldn't picture myself on either side at any of the tables.

I haven't walked very far, barely a hundred yards. I could easily have had some refreshments at the hotel, but the longer I stood by the window in my room, the more I thought it was worth visiting the little café down the street. It wasn't a spur-of-the-moment decision, as I had been standing there for some time watching people go by before I finally left the room. By then the sun had broken through the clouds and was shining on the buildings across the street, which undoubtedly made the café all the more enticing. The door was open, and from my window I could see the sun's rays penetrating inside. But sun or no sun, I had noticed that the people who went in seemed more cheerful when they came out again, in particular a young couple who held each other at length in a warm embrace on the sidewalk before parting. It wasn't easy to hug someone holding a coffee in a paper cup, and they laughed at their own clumsiness as they endeavored not to spill their drinks.

It's five o'clock. The sun is still shining but mostly on the roofs of the houses, leaving the street below in a cool shadow. Outside the hotel, a waiter is spreading cloths over the few tables arranged on the pavement and placing a small vase of cut flowers on each. I can tell straightaway he is experienced, although he can't be over thirty; I see it in the way he moves, with business-like precision and confidence—indeed, he gives the impression he could do his job with his eyes closed. I have always believed that being a good waiter is a question of temperament and can be only partially taught. This is why I long ago developed the strategy of interviewing potential waiters when there are no guests around, ideally between lunch and dinner services. All I ask them to do is set and then clear a table—whether for two or for eight, it makes no difference. Occasionally I ask them to behave as if there are people sitting at the table. This certainly used to raise a few eyebrows in the restaurant trade, I gather, where people are just as prone to gossiping as they are anywhere else.

But it's the young couple I feel the need to say more about, just to be clear. When I watched them emerge from the café and embrace holding their paper cups, it isn't that I thought of Miko and me. Not exactly, I have to say. Although I am quite sure we walked down this street more than once and might even have paused to embrace on the pavement when no one was looking. There was no café back then, and the hotel hadn't opened, though I don't remember what the building was used for. I wasn't really thinking of anything in particular when I stood by the window looking down on the street; I wasn't reminiscing or contemplating the future. In fact, it was one of those rare moments when the mind is quiet, able to enjoy what the eyes see without interpreting or destroying the moment with unnecessary speculation, when the eyes capture a ray of sunlight on a wall and direct it into the soul. I felt content and didn't want that blissful feeling to end. Which is why I stood for so long by the window looking out.

But now I have started thinking about her. And the fact is, I am not sure whether to open Facebook, because if she has sent me a message, I don't think I can read it without her knowing. I thought of contacting Sonja to check if this is true, as I did promise to let her know how my journey was going, and it occurred to me that I could ask her discreetly. But this is a bad idea, because she would ask why I wanted to know and whom it concerned. And besides, it's much too early for me to be getting in touch with Sonja. I should wait until I arrive in Japan or at least until I am well on my way.

Naturally I long to know if Miko has sent me a message. My fingers are itching to take out my phone and open Facebook in the hope that my heart will miss a beat. And yet fear is holding me back, the same fear that suddenly overwhelmed me mid-flight and which I seem unable to shrug off.

I started to think about what I would do if she told me not to visit her. I should mention that I haven't said a word to her about my plan, or in any way hinted at it, accidentally or otherwise. I am sure about this because I reread all our exchanges on Facebook before I went to sleep last night, precisely to make sure I hadn't foolishly given something away. My fears aren't entirely unjustified, however: I have good reason to be cautious, because Miko often seemed able to read my thoughts and didn't hesitate to tell me what they were if she thought it necessary.

I remember well the first time it happened. I had recently started, maybe it was even my first weekend.

"Why don't you have some more?"

"What do you mean?"

"You want seconds. Why not help yourself?"

It was after ten at night, the last guests had left, we were having a bite to eat after a busy shift—soba noodles with scallions and pork. She was right, I was thinking about having a second helping, but I was full and would soon be going to bed. Also, I didn't want to appear greedy.

"I don't need any more."

"But you want more . . ."

"I'm going home to bed. It's bad for my digestion."

"Are you already so old you can't handle a few extra noodles?"

"Miko," Takahashi-san said, "that's enough."

She continued to look at me with that half smile of hers, and I felt my face flush.

No, there is nothing strange about me wanting to be cautious. On the other hand, I don't see how I can put off much longer checking to see if she has sent me a new message. Because she still hasn't explained why they disappeared so suddenly, she hasn't told me what she has been doing for the past fifty years, only that she often thought of trying to find me but never did. She hasn't explained what stopped her.

The coffee is good. A little strong, but it has a sweet rather than a bitter taste, as the young barista rightly pointed out. She also said it had a cherry flavor, which I couldn't taste at first, but now I think I see what she means.

I don't regret crossing the street for the coffee. In fact, I am already thinking about having a second cup, as the decision about where to wander next is proving difficult. Maybe I should just leave it to chance, set off and go wherever my feet take me, starting perhaps by following the sun, which just started to shine on the little square down the street.

Jói Steinsson is responsible for my applying for a job with Takahashi-san at Nippon. We had met up at a pub close to campus; it was a Friday afternoon, as I recall. It was about a week after I told him and my other friends that I had decided to quit my studies, while at the same time condemning Western societies and commenting at length on the failure of economic models and theories. Some of my friends saw this as a bold gesture, as many of them held similar views, but now they had to admit, at least to themselves, that they didn't have the necessary courage to take a stand. But not Jói Steinsson. He just scoffed and said I would cool off in a week or two, or words to that effect. And then he changed the subject, as if he considered my news unworthy of further discussion.

I have sometimes wondered if I might not have changed my mind had Jói not put me in that situation. If he hadn't patronized me in that pub in front of our friends. Because Jói's words always had a sting in their tail, even though he pretended to be only teasing, a certain arrogance I couldn't stand.

I am not saying Jói is to blame for my decision to quit university and apply for a job as a "kitchen slave," as he put it. That would be as unwarranted as blaming him for being a superior student. But he just had this way of provoking me, though sometimes I suspect he was totally oblivious of it.

Anyway, as I was saying, Jói and I and two other friends were walking around this neighborhood, on a side street between the campus and Covent Garden, when Jói noticed a sign in a restaurant window asking for kitchen staff. While we weren't discussing my decision any longer, one of the boys had asked me earlier what I planned to do now that I had quit university, and I replied only that time would tell or something equally vague. That was all, and yet somehow this had clearly stayed with Jói, because suddenly, as if during the entire walk he had been waiting for the opportunity, he exclaimed: "Hey, look, Kristófer, maybe you could get a job there." I don't need to emphasize the deliberate mockery in his voice as he and our friends continued down the street, laughing at his joke. But I stopped in my tracks, pausing for a split second before pushing open the door to the restaurant and stepping inside.

I'm going to take the opportunity to mention that the entrance was two steps below street level and that the door had a glass panel so you could see inside. To the left of the door was a large window, which helped make it less gloomy. The lights were off when I walked in, the semi-darkness merging with the dense silence that greeted me. There was nobody about, and I might have been tempted to hurry out again if I hadn't noticed my friends, who had turned around and were hovering outside.

Only when I cleared my throat softly did Takahashi-san emerge from the kitchen. At first I was convinced I had woken him, which was probably true, as I later discovered he was in the habit of taking a nap after the lunch shift. He gave a little bow and said in a thick accent: "We open at six."

I explained why I was there. He looked me up and down and was about to send me away, he told me later, but for some reason hesitated. "Can you come at ten o'clock tomorrow morning?" he asked. "We can have a conversation then."

I agreed, although I had no intention of returning the next day and was going to tell my friends I had been turned down for the job. That would have shut Jói up, shown him that his sarcasm didn't affect me, his opinions didn't interest me, and I considered any job better than wasting my time on economics.

Indeed, I had already prepared my speech when I opened the door and walked straight into her. Instantly my mind went blank; a kind of noiseless explosion went off inside my head and knocked me out. Neither of us said a word, and I was too stunned even to apologize or hold the door open for her. She looked into my eyes as if she had seen something amusing and then smiled and darted inside.

I thought about her the rest of the day and also when I lay in bed that night and the following morning when I awoke to gentle rain. I remembered her smile, the gesture of her hand pushing her hair away from her face as she waited for me to let her pass, the electrical charge I felt when she brushed past me. Neither of us had said anything. She had looked into my eyes.

I realized I was being crazy. I felt afraid of having no control over my thoughts, yet I couldn't help it. There are millions of people in London, I said to myself. Millions of men and women. But then after a moment another voice responded: There are also millions of stars in the sky, but there's life on only one of them.

When I woke the next morning, I wasn't thinking about the cosmos anymore but rather that I might never see that girl again. For some reason I had assumed she worked at the restaurant or was maybe a regular, but now it occurred to me that there was no basis for that assumption. When I realized this, a bewildering sense of despair took hold of me, which was verging on panic by the time I left home for my job interview at Nippon.

I must say that I had no idea what to expect. Having never worked at a restaurant, I knew nothing about the way they functioned. Besides, there were almost no Japanese restaurants in London at the time; I knew of only one that had opened recently in Mayfair and was expensive. By contrast, Indian and Chinese restaurants were extremely popular, especially among young people who were tired of English cooking and more open to trying new things. I had been to a few myself, as the food was reasonably priced.

It shouldn't come as a surprise that I find myself now walking in the direction of the street where Nippon used to be. Indeed, it would be completely predictable were it not for the fact that I haven't been back there since I left London in the spring of 1970. During my many subsequent trips to the city, I saw no reason to visit, not even when Inga first came with me and asked me to show her some of my old haunts. I easily avoided going there then, as I had spoken very little to her about the months I spent at Nippon. Even so, I remember her asking about "that Japanese place" where I once worked, but when I told her it had closed down years ago, she didn't pursue it.

The sunshine is swiftly disappearing and present now only in the west-facing streets. The shadows lengthen, tinged with blue, and with them comes a sense of peace and stillness. I have meandered a little, and as I reach Seven Dials, I come to a halt and glance about, almost as if I am expecting to bump into myself at any moment, a young man on his way to a job interview. I am lost in my thoughts for a while, and when at last I recover my senses, I make a concerted effort and head straight up Short's Gardens.

I have just received a call from my doctor's office to inform me that my brain scan has been postponed. All non-emergency procedures are being suspended until further notice, the woman on the phone said. "Because of the virus," she explained when I didn't respond immediately, although it was obvious. I hesitated only because I thought they had already told me this and was about to ask her if I was right when thankfully I thought better of it. There is no need to give the doctor more reasons to speculate about my faculties.

I had just started along Short's Gardens when she called. I stopped while we spoke, as I find walking and talking at the same time somewhat uncomfortable. But I am walking again now and not far from my old place of work, five minutes at most.

It rained on my way to the interview. Not a downpour but that typical London drizzle, continuous and rather warm. I arrived early and took shelter down the street while I waited until it was ten o'clock. I watched a delivery van pull up and two men carry boxes into the corner shop across the road—what looked like canned food but also apples and oranges. Then they drove off and I was left watching the rain come down in the street.

I admit I was fully aware of the foolishness of my quest. I knew nothing about the job for which I was supposedly applying and had never had any desire to work at a restaurant, not until the day before, that is, and only then for all the wrong reasons, obviously.

Yes, I was fully aware of all that. I even said it to myself as I stood there counting the minutes. I scolded myself. I tried reasoning with myself. I was on the verge of turning around and hurrying home. But then I saw her in my mind's eye, half smiling, her fingers brushing her hair away from her forehead.

I saw no sign of her when I pushed open the door. Smells were coming from the kitchen, and I could hear the drone of a pop song merging with the clatter of pots and pans. I assumed they were singing in Japanese. This time I didn't need to clear my throat, because after only a few seconds Takahashi-san emerged from the kitchen. He bowed. I returned the gesture automatically. He smiled.

He was maybe in his mid-fifties, of medium height, slim and strongly built at the same time, with a few flecks of gray in his hair. We stood facing each other for a moment; the bar was on my left, next to the window looking out on the street, the kitchen straight ahead, the dining room on my right. He ushered me there, and we sat at one of the dozen or so tables, I with my back to the door.

I was thinking about how straight he sat in his chair when he started asking me questions. At first I had difficulty understanding him and turned bright red when I had to ask him to repeat himself, but then my ear became attuned.

He asked which restaurants I had worked at.

"None," I replied.

"So what do you do?" he asked.

I told him.

"You are quitting your studies at that university? That esteemed university?"

I nodded.

"Why?"

I tried to explain, but I could see he didn't understand what I was saying or else found it ridiculous. He frowned, even scowled a little, and after I had finished talking, he looked at me mutely. "What can you cook?" he then asked.

I was going to say "nothing" but then realized I could perhaps make something of my rather limited experience as a ship's cook on the seiner *Enok*.

"I can boil haddock and potatoes," I said, and told him about the fishing boat and the village of Patreksfjörður, where we had sailed from.

He sat up in his chair. "You've been to sea?"

"Yes," I said. "Four summers."

He asked what fish we caught on the seiner.

"Flatfish," I said, "mostly plaice but sometimes halibut. And a few monkfish, which nobody wanted."

"Wait," he said, "I'll be right back." He leaped to his feet, vanished into the kitchen, and came straight back holding an atlas. "Show me on the map."

"This is Patreksfjörður, here."

"How long were you out?"

"Overnight, sometimes longer if we sailed to Arnarfjörður," I said, showing him on the map.

"Good fish?"

"Very good."

He continued to scour the map as if searching for something.

"I also cooked leg of lamb," I added, feeling I was on a roll. "Roasted in the oven."

But he was interested only in the fish and wanted to know more about my time at sea. I told him I had also been on a hand-line boat out of Reykjavík, an old cutter; we had mostly fished in Selvogsbanki and Reynisdjúp, just off Pétursey.

"What?" he said. "What did you catch there?"

"Pollock," I said.

"Big ones?"

"Yes, seven or eight kilos."

He was clearly impressed by my experiences. I decided for good measure to tell him I had also worked on a trawler out of the Westman Islands back in the summer of '65.

"Was it a big boat?"

"A fifty-tonner," I told him. "We would sail in the evening and return three days later in the morning. We didn't get much sleep."

He asked me what fish we caught on the trawler.

"Mostly haddock," I said. "It feeds off the herring roe on the seabed. But sometimes we caught cod and plaice."

I showed him the Westman Islands on the map along with Selvogsbanki, Reykjavík, and Pétursey.

"Kristófer-san," he then said, "may I see your hands?"

I showed them to him, palms upturned, then the backs as well. He murmured softly as he contemplated them and then nodded as though confirming something to himself. Whatever it was, he didn't share it with me.

"I'm from a town by the sea," he said at last. "Can you start tomorrow?"

Tonkatsu, torikatsu, soba, tempura, donburi. Yakitori on Thursdays. *Okonomiyaki* on weekends. *Nanban soba, sansai soba, tsukimi soba* with egg yolk floating in the noodle soup like a full moon. Hence the name.

I wrote this down as I did everything else, in a little notebook which I bought after my first day at Nippon when I had only a loose scrap of paper on which to jot down the things Takahashi-san showed me or told me about. He was a patient teacher, as was Goto-san, the sous-chef, although his English was limited. *Saba*, mackerel. *Buta*, pork. *Unagi*, eel. *Tsukimi*, moon viewing.

Not that I needed to worry too much about cooking for the time being. I washed the dishes and helped clear the tables when the waitress needed me. Her name was Hitomi; she was probably approaching forty, petite and quick in her movements, and she didn't hesitate to address the English-speaking customers in Japanese when she felt it was appropriate, though they couldn't understand a word and she spoke perfectly good English. Later

I discovered this was mostly gentle teasing, "Aren't you going to finish your food?" and other such remarks. In any case, it was fairly obvious from her expression that she was only joking, and the customers always took it well.

There were no other staff on weekdays, as the restaurant was small and the menu simple. Takahashi-san took turns with Hitomi greeting customers, moving swiftly between the kitchen and the dining room. He took time to chat with his customers, especially his compatriots, the majority of them men who worked for Japanese companies in the city, in commerce, banking, insurance, shipping, car manufacturing. They and their families lived in places like Hampstead or Harrow-on-the Hill, Purley or East Croydon, and would come on weekdays to eat lunch or dinner, less frequently on weekends, when they would remain at home in the suburbs and play golf. At first they struck me as a rather uniform bunch of so-called salarymen, or regular office workers, but as I got to know them better, I realized they were as different from one another as everybody else.

When he started out, Takahashi-san had served mostly fish and chips as there was no demand for Japanese cuisine in London. Gradually, he added other seafood to the menu, but it was only in recent years, with the establishment of the Japanese business community in the city, that Nippon was born.

The kitchen was small and there wasn't much room to move. Yet I instantly felt at home in that cramped space, and the conditions didn't bother me at all, not the searing heat when they were cooking on all hobs and hot water flowed from the tap in front of me, not the small sink and the shelves crammed with dishes, not the low ceiling at my end of the kitchen where, for the first few days, I kept banging my head on the pipe protruding from the wall. No, none of it bothered me; I had worked in worse conditions at sea. None of it save the absence of the girl whom I had seen neither hide nor hair of since I walked into her in the doorway and resolved to turn my life upside down as a result.

That was on Monday. Two days later I started work. I didn't see her that day, or the day after, or when I came to work on Friday. Needless to say, I was anxious to find out more about her, to ask Takahashi-san or Hitomi who she was, but I couldn't find a way of doing that without giving myself away.

Across the kitchen door was a curtain that was usually drawn back halfway, giving a discreet view of the reception area and the customers as they arrived. Working by the sink, I was able to see out only if I stepped back a few paces toward the stove. But I also made regular trips from the kitchen to see if she was maybe sitting at one of the tables in the dining room, had slipped past without me noticing, alone or in company. But she was nowhere to be seen except in my mind, where her image had implanted itself and was so vivid, I might have been looking at her in a book or a magazine.

When Takahashi-san hired me, he told me I would have two days off a week but then asked if I could work the whole of the coming week without a break. Between the lunch and dinner services, from about three in the afternoon until six, I was free to do as I pleased. While Goto-san and Hitomi made themselves scarce, Takahashi-san took a nap on a bench in the pantry. But I didn't know what to do with myself, for it was precisely around that time of day when she had visited, and I couldn't risk missing her.

On my first day I sat at a table in the dining room reading, but the following afternoon, when Takahashi-san encouraged me to have a change of scenery, I took a stroll around the neighborhood, went into a record shop and a hardware store even though I didn't need anything. I stayed in the vicinity of Nippon, walked past it a few times and peered inside but saw nobody. On Friday I sat in a café on the corner where I could watch the street.

I would have made a dreadful spy, because when I returned to work at about half past five, the girl was already there and had started setting the tables in the dining room. She turned around when I opened the door, half smiling at me as she watched me come in. I stood motionless in the middle of the room and didn't even have the sense to take off my coat. And so we continued to contemplate each other until I managed to say hello, after what seemed like ages.

"So, you're the *gaijin* Dad was telling me about," she replied. "Hello."

This was a mistake. A predictable one, naturally, as there is a reason why I haven't come here in almost fifty years. I should point out, though, that I don't expect my memory of the place to be affected at all, for I can remember every last nook and cranny of Nippon, the facade included. It is indeed the facade that I happen to be looking at right now, and it's unrecognizable, as I might have expected. "Joe's Tattoo Parlor" is written above the door. The big window on the left is there, but the old door has been replaced with a steel one, painted black. The facade is gray and unappealing, as if the owners of the tattoo parlor are trying their hardest to keep prospective customers away.

When I first started to work at Nippon, the door was yellow and the facade light gray. But Miko found the colors ugly and persuaded Takahashi-san to let her paint the door dark blue and the walls light blue. I offered to help her, and we arrived at half past eight one Saturday morning in May, finishing the first coat by lunchtime and the second coat the following morning.

And now Nippon is a tattoo parlor. I have nothing against tattoos as such, although I generally find them rather unattractive, especially on women. Sonja has a different view, of course, and in fact became convinced that I disliked Axel because of the tattoos he has chosen to adorn himself with. To be clear, I don't dislike Axel, she's wrong about that. I thought he was a bit of a fool when they first started seeing each other; I would have preferred it if he had introduced himself to me and Inga after spending the night with Sonja instead of sneaking out through her bedroom window. But I didn't hold that against him, any more than I judged him because of his tattoos, although I did make the mistake once of bringing them up in conversation.

I think it only right to mention that Axel has a few tattoos and seems to have added to them over the years, not that I have been counting. But it was the design on his left arm that I allowed myself to ask him about. It has two sections, from the wrist to the elbow and from the elbow to the shoulder. The characters are Japanese, blue ink on the forearm and black on the upper arm. This was the first time Sonja brought him over to dinner with Inga and me. They wanted to come on a Saturday evening, which meant asking Baldur to cover for me at work. It was inconvenient for both him and me, but Inga was eager to please Sonja, so I decided not to raise any objections. Axel didn't try to hide his tattoos; on the contrary, he wore a T-shirt, although the weather wasn't particularly warm, and he appeared to be seeking attention or some commentary. As I said to Sonja afterward, when she flew off the handle: "It would have been rude of me not to mention them."

And so I asked him why he had chosen lettering, that lettering in particular.

"I thought it looked cool," he said. "I've always liked samurais and stuff like that."

"Are they qualities you especially admire?" I asked.

"What?" he said.

"Courage and fortitude," I said.

"Yeah, sure," he said.

Afterward Sonja said I knew perfectly well that Axel hadn't a clue what the writing on his arm meant and I had humiliated him with my questions. In response, I asked how I was supposed to know he would get a tattoo without understanding what it meant, it would never occur to me that anybody could be so . . .

"Be so what?" she asked when I trailed off mid-sentence.

"Well, I really don't know," I replied.

"Stupid?"

"I didn't say that."

She had the bit between her teeth, and there was no way to placate her.

"You're the only person I know who would ask the meaning of a tattoo," she said. "They are just decorative. And how do you know what it meant? Since when do you speak Japanese?"

I explained they were well-known designs, familiar to anybody who had some knowledge of Japanese culture. Thankfully she didn't ask me any more questions, as she had grown tired of the conversation.

Inga insisted I had only myself to blame and that if I had kept my mouth shut, Sonja probably would have grown tired of Axel at some point. Inga had nothing against Axel and said this only to needle me. But that was later, shortly after they married, and while I don't recall the exact context, her words stung and have obviously stayed with me.

Axel is a bit of an entrepreneur. He has owned a couple of gyms and a self-storage business, a wire mesh company and a car dealership. He seems to have a good nose for business and has done pretty well for himself. He drives flashy cars, and whenever he buys a new one, he makes a point of coming around to show it to me. I don't think he is trying to tell me something, his mind doesn't work like that, he just seems to genuinely believe that I am a car enthusiast. Maybe I once commented on one of his cars out of politeness because, all in all, I feel rather sorry for the poor guy. But I have no interest in cars, which he should have understood by now.

Miko painted the door and the window frames while I concentrated on the wall. We had good weather both days, and the sun shone down on us all morning. I still hadn't told her how I felt about her and wasn't sure I would ever get the chance. I can remember reflecting about that during those mornings, as I observed her out of the corner of my eye, her look of concentration, her delicate gestures, the sun on her ebony hair. I remember I didn't feel very hopeful.

Once she suddenly turned around while I was letting myself daydream.

"What exactly are you looking at?" she asked, her lips curved in a half smile. I turned bright red and hurriedly dipped my brush in the paint can.

I move closer to the building, because all of a sudden I think I can see a patch where the gray paint has peeled off. Upon closer inspection it turns out I am right, and my heart leaps unexpectedly when I spy the blue paint beneath. I'm getting ready to pull off some loose flakes when I stop myself and step back a few paces. There I contemplate the house for the last time before walking away, resolved not to turn around or even look back over my shoulder.

I am sitting outside a small restaurant near Covent Garden. Looking around, I gather that roughly every other table is occupied. The temperature has dropped; however, the outdoor heaters between the tables are doing their job, so I don't feel cold. I am not too hot either, because the waiter took great care when adjusting the flame. He told me he could turn it up if it turned colder, as the heater closest to me is only on medium.

I open Facebook. After giving it more thought, I have decided to respond truthfully if, as I suspect, she has a hunch about my trip. I have also decided to continue my journey come what may, and not to let her talk me out of it, whatever her objections. I already have my glasses on my nose, as I needed them to read the menu, so checking the phone requires minimal effort.

In my last message, sent yesterday, I asked her straight out to tell me what actually happened. I have been skirting the issue since she first contacted me, and I couldn't stay silent any longer. Naturally, I was careful to pose the question in such a way that it wouldn't upset her, and I double-checked before sending that I hadn't said anything that might make her feel guilty, directly or indirectly. If anything, I attempted to make light of the matter, although I am not sure if that came across.

She has responded. About four hours ago, I gather. While I was on my way to the hotel, a short distance away if I got the timing right, probably just as I was turning onto Tottenham Court Road. Not that it matters, yet somehow it makes me feel better to know exactly where I was when she was writing to me. It would have been about midnight her time, though she didn't say so in her message.

In brief, she didn't reply to my question. Nor did she ignore it, but she apologized for feeling too weak just now. "I'm not trying to wriggle out of anything," she added. "Hopefully tomorrow."

I reread all our messages to make sure none of them had dissolved in my head. From the first through to the last. There is no need, but maybe the doctor has me doubting myself. I resent him for this and am beginning to think I can do without his help. At least I got out of having the MRI scan.

This is what her messages have revealed: She has been living in Japan since their departure from London. She lives alone. Takahashi-san died about twenty years ago, at a ripe old age. She has been a secondary school teacher all her working life, up until she retired a few years ago. Many times she resolved to get in touch with me, but she never got around to it. She hopes I have had a good life. She herself can't complain.

"We were so young," she wrote in two of her messages and left it at that. For my part I am unsure whether to interpret those words as a justification for her and her father's disappearance or as some kind of explanation.

She also tells me that she reads a lot and has recently taken up knitting. She loves to dance. Her flat is close to the city center. She hasn't been to England since "that time."

I try to imagine her saying aloud what she writes in her messages. As if the two of us are sitting in the café next to her university one quiet afternoon. I try to envision her before me, to hear her voice, to decide whether these words correspond to her.

Gaijin. That was what she called me at first. Not only on the Friday, when I encountered her setting tables in the dining room, but also later. I looked it up and discovered it's something the Japanese call Westerners—white people, in other words—and doesn't have to be derogatory. It comes from the word *gai*, meaning "outside," and *jin*, meaning "man." *Gaijin* is therefore somebody who stands outside. But Takahashi-san objected to her calling me that and scolded her whenever he overheard her, so she just made sure he didn't.

"*Gaijin*," she said, "is it true you quit your studies to be able to wash dirty dishes?"

She herself was a student at UCL and worked at her father's restaurant only on weekends; she arrived on Fridays after her lectures, worked both shifts on Saturdays, and left after lunch on Sundays to spend time on her studies. Over the summer holidays she got a job at one of the university laboratories and continued to work shifts at the restaurant. She covered for Hitomi, who had the weekends off, like Goto-san, who was replaced by a forty-something British man called Steve. Both Hitomi and Goto-san came back to work the evening shift on Sundays.

I had two days off, variously on Monday, Tuesday, or Wednesday. My replacements were two men who worked at other restaurants and moonlighted to supplement their wages. Incidentally, Takahashi-san said he was aware that young men like me preferred to have the weekends off, and he would see what he could do. Obviously, that idea didn't appeal to me at all, and I assured him that Mondays and Tuesdays suited me better, or Wednesdays, and that I would rather work on weekends. He was happy with the arrangement.

The first weekend she and I worked together is still fresh in my memory. She was busy waiting tables, though of course she came into the kitchen regularly with the customers' orders, to fetch them when they were ready and to bring me the dirty dishes. Most often wordlessly, but sometimes our hands would touch, and then I blazed like an oven. I reproached myself and then immediately found myself waiting for her to bring more dirty dishes and cutlery, maybe to make a witty remark in passing, to brush against me.

On Saturday evening my first weekend, one table stayed late. These were three couples having a good time, drinking beer and sake after their meal, and appeared to have lost track of time. Goto-san had already left, and Miko was counting the takings at the till while Takahashi-san used the opportunity to take stock in the pantry. When they finished their tasks, I noticed that Miko was growing restless. She had started to look pointedly at the clock and then she declared: "Isn't it time these people left," or something like that. Although she said it in a whisper, Takahashi-san hushed her anyway, reminding her that customers were welcome to stay as long as they wanted. Maybe she didn't roll her eyes, but she made it quite clear it was time for them to leave.

"Why are you in such a hurry?" Takahashi-san asked.

"Elizabeth and Penny are waiting for me. We're meeting up with some other students."

"I was thinking of going home," he said. "I was going to ask if you could lock up."

Had I known him better, I would have seen through this ploy, because Takahashi-san was always the last to leave. He could have let his daughter go if he wanted, but something was stopping him.

But I was naive and offered to help, mostly to look good in Miko's eyes.

"I can clear the table and clean up after they leave," I said. "I'm not in any hurry."

"You're new here," Takahashi-san said, and then after a brief hesitation, he added with a sigh: "Oh, very well."

She smiled at me, gave her father a peck on the cheek, and then she was gone.

The customers stayed for another fifteen minutes or so. Takahashi-san seemed pensive but said nothing more about his daughter. Until we walked out together—then, all of a sudden, he muttered as he was locking the door behind us: "These young people."

I felt rather pleased that he had excluded me, only to discover a few days later which young people he was referring to. But then I felt so dejected that I scarcely gave another thought to Takahashi-san and his reaction.

The waiter is clearing my table when my phone emits a noise indicating that I have a new text message. We had been discussing the heater, which he had just turned up, and the virus, which is on everybody's mind. He had offered me some hand sanitizer when he brought my food over, explaining that he had disinfected my cutlery and thought I might want to do my hands. But now my phone is buzzing, and I pick it up as the waiter walks away.

It's Mundi. He is unfortunately somewhat relentless about text messaging and has gotten worse lately. Sometimes he sends me a joke he finds funny or an article he wants me to read, other times his own thoughts or opinions, which aren't always intelligible. The following message belongs to the category of thoughts and opinions: "It's inedible, just as I expected."

I recall our last conversation, but I can't think of what he is referring to.

"The fish cakes. The idiot used the leftovers from last night."

Now it comes back to me, the fish he was complaining to

me about. I decide not to respond. I don't like this way of com-
municating; I find it impossible to have a conversation via text
message, and besides, it takes me forever to type. I don't see how
Mundi manages with those great paws of his, but then he isn't
too bothered by typos.

Naturally, he isn't put off. "Where are you?"

I tell him.

"Weren't you going to Japan." (Or rather: "Wern t you hong
ti japn.")

"Tomorrow," I reply after a lengthy pause. But my delayed
response doesn't deter Mundi, who responds as fast as his fingers can type.

"Why didn't you let Baldur take over the restaurant?"

This arrives like a bolt from the blue and gets my back up
immediately, as I have long been fed up with Mundi's meddling.

"What are you talking about?"

"He is disappointed that you didn't offer it to him."

I am utterly exasperated. My brother has evidently been in
touch with Baldur to see if he is already working at another restaurant. His motives are apparent: Mundi is pestering my former employee because he wants food delivered.

I refuse to discuss this via text message. In fact, I refuse to
discuss it full stop, as it's none of Mundi's business how I run my
restaurant. Moreover, I won't permit him to speak on behalf of a
man who has worked for me for nearly fifteen years.

I am tempted to call Mundi and give him a piece of my mind,
but I am not in the mood. And yet his words have upset me, and
it is difficult for me to push them aside.

Was Baldur hoping to take over Torg? Did we ever discuss
that? No. Not that I recall. Of course, he has been my right-
hand man in recent years, and I have nurtured him as well as I
could, taught him all I have learned during my many years in the
business, believed in him, supported him to the best of my abil-

ity, especially when he had to give up drinking. He stayed the course, and on more than one occasion I accompanied him to A.A. meetings at his request, listening to him and others talk about their problems. I was happy to do it because I believed we had a close relationship. And then Mundi throws this at me.

Baldur and I never discussed what might happen after I eventually retired. Not in any serious way. Naturally, I alluded occasionally to the fact that I wouldn't be running the place forever, that I was getting older, even if people tend to think I am younger than I actually am. I often told him he was doing an excellent job, encouraged him when he complained that he didn't want to stagnate, made clear how much I appreciated him. Especially after his struggle with alcohol and when he was trying to get back on track. He certainly needed a lot of support and encouragement.

Yet I never discussed with him the possibility of him taking over from me, and if I am honest, he should be grateful to me for that. Running a restaurant is an endless struggle. Even in good times. Nothing can go wrong, no detail can be missed, every last penny counts. Often you will start the day with practically no reservations for that evening. Three or four tables maybe, that's it. And just as you are contemplating the empty tables on your computer screen, one of your suppliers calls to tell you they are raising their prices. Or you get a message from an employee who can't come to work. Or a bad review on Tripadvisor from a customer who was probably in a bad mood on the evening he ate at your restaurant and decided to take it out on you.

No, running a restaurant isn't the right job for Baldur. Not with his weaknesses. Although he has fallen off the wagon only once since he got sober, trouble is just a drink away. Alcoholism is like a hidden blaze. That's what people say.

I must not permit Mundi to upset me like this. He has done it once again, and I am kicking myself for it. It's enough for me to remember Baldur's speech at our last supper to know that Mundi is only stirring up trouble, to put it bluntly.

When Baldur stood up in the middle of the meal that last evening to take the floor, his speech was directed at me. Baldur is a sensitive soul, but he normally manages to keep his emotions under control. On this occasion, however, he didn't try to hold back but spoke from the heart. He repeated several times how grateful he was to me, described how I had taken him under my wing, guided and encouraged him, presented him with "the keys to the kitchen" when Ásberg left, stood by him when he was in recovery.

"It's no accident that I named my son after you, Kristófer, no accident at all."

I felt uncomfortable, but I stood up, clapped him on the back, and, sensing the atmosphere needed lightening, I jested: "Thankfully, it's only his middle name."

But the staff was still affected by Baldur's speech and my joke fell flat, and then we both sat down to tuck into our steak, which, it goes without saying, was cooked to perfection. And I said that to him too. I said so everybody could hear: "You never miss a beat."

I am not trying to make myself look good. Everything I did for Baldur, he deserved. And yet I am frankly shocked that he would give my brother this ammunition to use against me. Shocked and disappointed.

I had planned to have coffee and dessert, but my appetite has vanished, and I ask the waiter to bring me the bill. My phone buzzes after I have stood up and am heading back to the hotel, but rather than reach for it, I resolve to ignore Mundi for the remainder of my journey.

On my first day off, my second Tuesday at Nippon, I happened to be in central London in the afternoon. I had been hanging out with two university friends over lunch, listening to music and talking about football, but then went shopping for a pair of shoes and batteries for my transistor radio. Eventually we ended up in a bookstore off Oxford Street, where I somehow found a Japanese book for beginners in the discount bin and started leafing through it. I was about to put it down when I told myself it wouldn't be a bad idea for me to acquaint myself a bit with the language. The book was inexpensive, so I really didn't need to think twice. I remember one of my friends opening it at random while we were waiting to pay and trying to pronounce some sentence or other. They were the two boys who were with Jói Steinsson and me the day I applied for the job at Nippon, so I didn't need to explain to them my reason for buying it.

"*'Eigo o hanasemasu ka*,'" he read, and then gave the translation: "Do you speak English?"

That was when I heard a familiar voice behind me.

"Are you going to learn Japanese, Kristófer? Then we can't talk behind your back anymore."

I swung around. There she stood with two books in her hands and a young man beside her, clearly having been watching us. I was flustered but quickly collected myself, and before I could stop myself, I retorted: "Would you like to borrow it?"

She was taken aback, and I could see immediately that my reply had struck home. The truth was that Takahashi-san had remarked more than once that his daughter didn't speak good enough Japanese, that she had become English and was in danger of losing her roots. He wasn't shy about saying this to her in front of me and the other staff, and when the two of us were alone, he had urged me not to lose my Icelandic, while admitting he should have done more to ensure that his daughter kept up with her mother tongue. I was never sure how serious he was about this, as sometimes he seemed to be simply teasing Miko, reminding her in a good-natured way not to forget where she came from. She would respond in kind, saying things like "Oh, Dad" or just rolling her eyes. But now when I looked at her face, I realized how deeply his remarks had affected her. The smile vanished from her lips immediately, as did the mocking twinkle in her eyes. It was as if I had stripped her of an invisible shield, leaving her standing exposed before me.

It all happened in a few seconds and she soon rallied, tried to smile again and then decided to introduce me to her friend. "Naruki, this is Kristófer. He quit his studies at the LSE to wash dishes for my dad."

We shook hands.

"Don't forget the cutlery," I added in the same tone as before, and then I introduced them to my friends.

There wasn't time for anything else, as I was next in the

queue. I paid for my book, and seconds later my friends and I had left the shop.

It is unthinkable that I would have responded to her in that way had I been on my own. I simply would have spluttered and stammered while she pressed her advantage and carried on with her banter—at my expense. But I was emboldened by my friends, or I felt compelled to show off in front of them.

But I mustn't forget to mention Naruki and how his presence affected me. They weren't holding hands or being affectionate toward each other, and yet the nature of their relationship was clear. My heart sank the moment I saw him, which undoubtedly governed my reaction as well.

I would have assumed Takahashi-san was pleased with such a match, that he preferred Miko to associate with a man of Japanese origin, and yet seemingly that wasn't the case. I instantly thought of the scene that Saturday night when he had tried to stop her from going out with "her friends" and saw it now in a different light. I found it odd that Takahashi-san should be meddling in his twenty-two-year-old daughter's life, but I attributed it to cultural differences, for in many ways Takahashi-san was strict and old-fashioned, despite having lived in England since Miko was two. That was more or less everything I knew about their past at that point.

I waited for Friday with both longing and trepidation. I had started to put my free time between lunch and dinner to better use and would occasionally go back to the room I had rented after I moved out of the dorm. I would listen to music, read, or meet friends at a café if they weren't busy. I would arrive back at work before six, as there was always something to do, even though the dishwashing didn't start properly until later.

But that Friday I stayed around the neighborhood and returned shortly before five. I remember it was pouring rain and that I just made it inside before it started. I folded the tea towels in the kitchen, fetched some dishwashing liquid from the storage room, chatted briefly with Steve, who loved to talk about football. He was a big Arsenal fan, while I was a Leeds supporter.

I happened to be holding a tea towel when I saw her dash across the street. I had gone out to look for her through the window, not for the first time. She rushed in gasping for breath, her hair and her blue knee-length coat sopping wet. I handed her the tea towel. "Do you want to dry yourself?"

She took it from me silently and started to wipe her face, then patted her hair dry, calmly, undisturbed by me standing there watching her. When I saw she was ready to take off her coat, I held out my hand and took the towel from her.

"Thanks," she said.

I nodded and made to return to the kitchen.

"*Taoru,*" she said then.

"What?" I replied.

"Tea towel. *Taoru.*"

I gave a start, for I thought she was rebuking my behavior at the bookshop, showing me she didn't have a problem with her mother tongue. But then she smiled, stepped toward me, touched my arm for a brief moment, just above my elbow, and left me standing in the middle of the room as she continued into the kitchen.

There was a little yard out back with access via a door between the kitchen and the pantry, through the broom closet. In reality, the yard was more like an alleyway bordered by six-foot-high walls separating it from the strips of garden belonging to the adjacent houses and those backing onto us. On the right as you went out was a small round table with two chairs, and on the left a large refrigerator we used for excess food and drink that couldn't be accommodated inside. Next to the fridge were some crates containing fizzy drinks and beer.

When the weather was good, the sun shone into the yard for a while in the morning and then again in the afternoon. Goto-san liked to sit at the table and smoke, and sometimes he would fall asleep there. Takahashi-san and Hitomi seldom went out back unless they were fetching something from the fridge.

It was on Saturday. I could still feel her touch twenty-four hours after she had come in from the rain. We hadn't spoken to each other again after that; the restaurant was busy and she left as soon as we closed. She behaved neutrally. I didn't notice any change.

Recently I had started to sit outside when the weather permitted, and would take my transistor radio with me. It was dry, quite warm, the air was still. Every once in a while, the sun shone through the clouds. The lunch shift was over. Takahashi-san had gone out. Steve was in the kitchen.

I was listening to the sports news when Miko came outside. She had removed her apron and was wearing a black skirt and a white blouse. She paused where the sun shone down into the yard. I had my feet up on the empty chair and quickly took them off. She noticed but didn't move.

"Why did you stop?"

"Stop what?"

"Studying."

"I lost interest."

"Other people lose interest in their studies but still graduate."

"Not me."

"So you were interested at some point?"

"Yes."

"What happened?"

I realized I couldn't bring myself to repeat the same speech I had given others about the state of the world or the failure of economics. "Something changed."

"Dad doesn't understand you."

"My parents don't either," I said.

She looked at me. "And you? Do you understand yourself?"

I wasn't sure how to respond, and she didn't wait for me to reply.

"Sometimes I don't understand myself at all," she said.

"Isn't that uncomfortable?"

"No, I find it exciting."

I was going to ask what it was she didn't understand, but I

changed my mind. She lit a cigarette for herself; I had never seen her smoke, and I never would again. She held out the packet to offer me one, but I declined.

She was studying psychology. Her father had told me this and asked what I thought she could do with such a degree. I said I knew nothing about it, and I could see this disappointed him. He said he wished she had chosen a different subject. Something more practical. "She needs to be able to support herself," he said. "Not to depend on anybody."

It surprised me that Takahashi-san was so modern in this thinking. Although ignorant about Japanese society, I knew it wasn't exactly the cradle of feminism.

She looked at me as she smoked in silence. "You remind me of him," she said.

I didn't know whom she meant, but then she motioned toward the radio, on which John Lennon was singing "Julia." I hadn't noticed.

"It's just the beard," I said.

"No, there's something else."

I waited, but she offered no further explanation. "They're married now," she said instead. I nodded.

"Did you see the photos of them this morning?"

I told her I had. The news coverage of Lennon and Yoko Ono had been nonstop since they had commenced their bed-in for world peace in an Amsterdam hotel room two days before.

"What do you think?"

I said I thought they were doing a good thing, or words to that effect.

"No, I mean what do you think of them?"

I became a bit tongue-tied because suddenly I thought she might be insinuating something about the two of us. My heart leaped and hope flared in my chest. I was going to say something flattering about them, but she anticipated me.

"You know this song is about his mom."

Seashell eyes, windy smile, Lennon was singing.

"She abandoned him when he was a little boy," she went on. "Yoko Ono is his mom now."

I assumed she was joking and I grinned.

"Seriously," she said. "But I'm not like her."

She stubbed out her cigarette, threw the end in the rubbish bin by the door, and went inside.

Intimacy. That was the essence of Sonja's obituary about her mother. The unifying theme, at any rate, as the word came up several times. I might have said warmth, but Sonja used the word "intimacy," which she didn't need to ask permission from anybody to do, least of all me. Sonja often speaks in that way—about the inner core, being the best version of ourselves we can be—and she doesn't take kindly when I allow myself to joke gently about her choice of words. "Why not the super-deluxe version?" I said to her once. "Or the limited edition?" She wasn't amused. Anyhow, as I was saying, the essence of her obituary was intimacy, the role it plays in relationships. Some people need it more than others, she wrote, some people can't be happy without it. Inga had thrived on intimacy and been exceedingly generous, Sonja insisted, and went on to connect it with her mother's love of gardening, recalling how she talked to her flowers long before that kind of thing became fashionable. "Hers were the most beautiful of all; everybody who saw her peonies, for example, couldn't help but admire them. She gave away many cuttings that blossomed into magnificent plants but none could compete with her own." This charming much-repeated tale naturally became a little inflated with time, not that I wish to belittle Inga's peonies, which were surely a sight for sore eyes. Sonja ended the flower anecdote by declaring that Inga's love had paid dividends, for her blooms had given as much to her as she gave to them.

There was nothing wrong with the story, it was heartfelt and tastefully written, even if Sonja couldn't resist peppering it with clichés. In fact, there was nothing in the article I objected to until she began equating flowers and people. At that moment I winced, took off my glasses, and put them back on, imagining that I had fallen asleep while reading and was now in the middle of a dream.

"But flowers aren't like people and Mom knew this only too well."

The sentence might not have hit quite so hard if, say, Sonja had gone on to talk about Inga's sensitivity, her tendency to take so much in life to heart, things most people would shrug off. Not to mention her worst days, because, naturally, people's worst days have no place in an obituary.

Sonja could have done that perfectly well instead of writing the following, without even a paragraph break: "Mom was married twice. Her first husband was my father, Orri Gestsson, the photographer. They married very young—too young, Mom used to say—and although they were in love they grew apart and divorced when I was four years old. It's a tribute to their maturity that I was never aware of any conflict between them, and scarcely suffered either before or after their divorce, indeed my father cared for me just as if nothing had happened. My mother's second husband, my stepfather, is Kristófer Hannesson, a restaurant owner. He survives her."

Full stop. No other mention of me in the entire obituary. Then, after a paragraph break, this:

"Not everybody is capable of self-compassion. Mindfulness doesn't spring from nowhere. Without it there is no intimacy."

Despite the obituary going on to say something about how "none of us" had possessed Inga's generosity, "none of us" her "inner wellspring," the barbed comment was obviously aimed at me.

She left the subject of Hveragerði until the end. Her pen was running away with her by then, and she was rambling about this and that, no doubt because she was out of time. Sonja has a habit of leaving things to the last minute. I would often arrive home after a long day's work to find her still up after Inga had gone to bed, struggling to reach an essay deadline, cramming for an exam, invariably in a state of nerves. Exhausted as I was, I frequently sat up with her, reading over what she had written, helping her with a difficult math problem, correcting her work, offering advice, occasionally until after midnight. I don't recall her ever going to ask her photographer father, Orri, for help at those moments. I don't recall lacking in intimacy or generosity those nights.

I bore no resentment toward her, because her mother's death came as a devastating blow to her, as it did to me. I saw nothing to be gained from discussing her mother's problems with her, the off days I mentioned, and besides, Sonja had never wanted to know too much about them, and I had done my best to shield her. They grew more frequent after Sonja flew the nest and it was just the two of us; then Inga went through a bad time. But things gradually improved, especially after her rehab.

When Sonja and I embraced after the funeral service and followed the coffin out of the church, I thought I would never have to hear her say things like that again. Not at the wake, where she thanked me especially for having arranged everything so well, the food, the table decorations, the choice of music; not during the days that followed, when she would ring me several times a day to talk about her mother, to ask me this or that, to remember the good times. So it came as a complete surprise when she called me one evening two weeks later just to tell me I hadn't cried at the funeral.

I am wondering why this has come back to me now, out of the blue. All I can think of is that I have allowed the messages from Miko—which I have been rereading since I got back to my hotel room—to throw me off balance, to create a blaze where there wasn't even a spark before. I am specifically referring to her message from two days ago, which she wrote in the middle of the night her time and which, innocuous as it seems, I can't get out of my mind. In it she mentioned teaching, which she enjoyed; her husband, about whom I know nothing other than that he would have made a wonderful father; and then she concluded with these words: "But I've had a good life."

I was as happy to read that two days ago as I am to reread it now, and yet I am a bit pensive. I think back to the strange obituary and ask myself: Did Inga have a good life? I am unable to answer that question—everything is so gray and vague that I am inclined to think the doctor might be right. But then I rally and tell myself that of course Miko hasn't been happy simply because she decided to disappear and Inga wasn't unhappy because she spent all those years with me; of course I am imagining all these things simply to torment myself. I repeat this over and over, and although I know it's true, the doubts keep seeping into my mind like water into a boat, finding fresh cracks even as the old ones close, drop by drop, until suddenly I have the impression I am about to go under.

There is nothing like a good night's sleep.

I must have been exhausted after my journey, because I slept like a log and didn't wake up until almost seven o'clock, calm and completely rested. Before I even opened my eyes, I could feel that all the inner tensions had evaporated, been weeded out, and important events put in their proper context. I was relieved but at the same time a little disconcerted, for it felt exactly as if someone had entered my head while I was sleeping and done a thorough spring clean, rearranged everything, washed, dusted, and thrown away what belonged in the rubbish.

I can't say this clarity came from outside, because there is a constant drizzle and everything looks gray. While I was still dozing, I thought I heard the distant clang of cutlery and murmur of voices and briefly imagined I was dreaming about Torg, which I have occasionally over the years. Then I realized the sounds were coming from outside, and when I opened the bathroom window,

I found myself looking down on a neat backyard where breakfast was being served.

I am sitting there now, beneath the tarpaulin they have erected above the tables and chairs sheltering the four of us, seated at three tables, from the fine rain that, by the way, doesn't appear to affect the waiters. I have ordered bacon, eggs, black pudding, and toast, because I awoke feeling famished, as if I had been hard at work all night. Also, the aroma of bacon floating up had whetted my appetite when I opened the bathroom window, so I quickly shaved and brushed my teeth and, before I knew it, was hurrying downstairs.

It was Mundi's texts that rattled me. They upset me to the extent where I could no longer see things in proportion and quite frankly lost control of myself. One thing led to another, which is what happens when you go off course, one foolish thought after another, until I had painted myself into such a tight corner, I felt there was no way out. Fortunately, I am over it now, and the day ahead looks bright.

My thoughts turned to Takahashi-san when the waiter brought over my food. That is to say, the day he told me he was considering opening for breakfast, two mornings a week to begin with, on Wednesdays and Fridays, and asked if I felt ready to do a couple of extra shifts. He planned to open at seven, he said, and the prepping would be fairly simple, so I needn't arrive until half past five. I had experience with getting up at the crack of dawn from my days on the fishing boats, and besides have always been a lark, so this suited me fine. He went on to say that my tasks would be more varied than normal, because he wanted me to help him with the cooking.

Obviously I jumped at the offer. I had already started to help out with the prepping and was getting quite good at slicing veg-etables, making egg batter and cleaning fish, although I wasn't trusted yet to steam the rice or make stock. But I would learn those things with Takahashi-san, because the traditional Japanese breakfast follows the same formula as other meals, namely *ichiju sansai*: one soup, three dishes, consisting of miso soup, rice, pickled mixed vegetables, and grilled fish, normally salmon.

It was during those mornings that I felt I first got to know Takahashi-san, who was otherwise remarkably good at not talking about himself. Maybe I've been a bit influenced by him, it's quite possible, which would explain why Sonja implied in the obituary that I didn't give enough of myself. He and I spoke about every subject under the sun, which isn't unusual in restaurant kitchens, where people work side by side for long periods of time. We also both appreciated being alone for the first hour with nobody to interrupt our conversation or the silence, which was as agreeable as our talks. Takahashi-san extolled the benefits of "rising before dawn," and I agreed, because sometimes I feel daybreak stimulates something in the mind which I might otherwise not think of or at least might leave unsaid. I don't mean secrets, but thoughts one might not be aware of at other times of the day, or which might present themselves in a different guise.

I remember one morning I was slicing tofu for the miso soup when Takahashi-san said out of the blue: "Maybe I made a mistake."

I thought he meant with the cooking, though I didn't notice anything was amiss.

"When I moved here," he added.

I asked him when that was.

"Nineteen forty-eight."

"Don't you like it here?"

He was filleting salmon, and I had briefly set aside my knife to follow his swift, precise movements.

"I married late," he said without stopping what he was doing. "Don't marry late, Kristófer-san. Raising children is not a job for old men."

Obviously he was referring to Miko, and my cheeks flushed, because although he didn't mention her by name, I felt suddenly afraid he had discovered how I felt about her. I had done my utmost not to look at her in a way that might raise suspicions, but even so I turned bright red when I thought he had caught me out.

I felt I should say something, but nothing came to mind. He broke the silence: "Maybe I should have gone somewhere else. Maybe I should have stayed where I was."

"Do you have family here?"

"No."

"Why did you choose England?"

He smiled. "It was the cheapest flight."

I had never heard the family talk about where they lived in Japan, and I decided to ask where they came from.

"Tokyo," he answered.

"That's where you lived?"

"The flight left from there."

I didn't have the impression he was exactly avoiding my question, at least not from his tone, and yet something prevented me from probing any further. I grilled the salmon he had filleted and sliced, and soon afterward Hitomi arrived, and then our first customers.

That was on Friday. After lunch I sat at the table in the backyard with a cup of coffee and my book and waited for Miko to come. I had been working at Nippon for about six weeks then, and rather than leave the premises on Fridays and Saturdays between lunch and dinner, I would await her arrival with anticipation. Actually that wait commenced the moment her lunch shift finished on Sundays, when I instantly started to miss her. Twice on my days off I had even gone out of my way to walk past her university campus, without running into her, unsurprisingly. But there I was, waiting, glancing occasionally at my book, drinking the coffee I had made for myself, and watching the cotton-wool clouds drift by in the gentle southerly breeze.

I must have dozed off, because it took a while for me to realize it was Takahashi-san's voice reaching me in the yard. I had never heard him raise his voice before, and although he wasn't shouting, he was clearly upset. He was speaking mostly in Japanese, so I didn't understand what he was saying, but I could tell he was both angry and disappointed. Nor did I know to whom he was talking, as I heard no other voices, until Miko answered him at last with the words: "I'm not a child!"

There followed a heavy silence, and then the door into the yard opened and a second later Miko appeared. She paused just outside the door as though incapable of walking any farther and buried her face in her hands. I had never seen her in such a state, and I felt I had no right to, because she clearly hadn't noticed me. I cleared my throat and leaned back in my chair so that it creaked, but I didn't say anything. She jumped and took her hands away from her face, managing to first wipe her eyes quickly.

I longed to say something to her and yet I felt rather ashamed, as if I had been spying on her. I was even afraid she might be angry with me, but I needn't have been. She was silent, stared straight ahead without looking at me at first, then took a deep breath and said, perhaps to herself rather than to me: "He just doesn't understand."

I was about to ask what she meant but had the sense to keep quiet.

"I spoke to my professor about it," she said. "Twenty years and he is still stuck in the past. He acts like we're still there. Like we never left."

"Tokyo?"

She turned toward me, contemplated me, and then said after a brief pause: "No, Hiroshima."

I realized that she was telling me something significant. It troubled me that I had no idea what.

Although I had read about the nuclear attack on Hiroshima in school, my knowledge of the subject was limited to less than a page in a textbook. Maybe I didn't need to know more; maybe Miko was simply telling me that Takahashi-san was still struggling with the aftermath and had difficulty exorcising the ghosts of the past. This could hardly come as a surprise even to people like me, who knew so little of the history. However, I wasn't satisfied with that explanation alone, and in my mind, I kept looking at Miko turning toward me in the backyard and studying me before finally revealing the name of the city I had never heard her or her father mention before. Unwaveringly, I might add, for it wasn't as if she had carelessly blurted it out in the heat of the moment but, rather, decided to confide in me after some thought—though without any explanation.

I was registered at the university until spring and therefore still had access to the library. I headed there the following

Monday after lunch and began plowing through reports about the attack itself, the events leading up to it, and the aftermath. I learned that, among other reasons, Americans had chosen Hiroshima since it was by the sea and had escaped being attacked up until then. Tokyo had also been in the running, but because it had already sustained heavy damage, the destruction wrought by the atomic bomb would have been less dramatic. Hiroshima, on the other hand, was completely intact; the houses still stood, the bridge over the River Motoyasugawa, the main railway station, the port, the temple on Teramachi Street. People went to work in the morning, children went to school, the sun came up, and the sun went down. All that changed as if by a wave of the hand on August 6, 1945, at eight-fifteen in the morning. Then the bomb code-named "Little Boy" exploded approximately two thousand feet above the city and laid it to waste. More than seventy thousand people lost their lives that day, and the number would double in the months that followed.

This is what I read in the library and much more; in fact, I lost track of time and had to run back so as not to arrive late for my evening shift. I pored over a book with photographs of buildings and people taken before and after the attack. I tried to imagine Takahashi-san in those photographs. I didn't succeed.

I felt worse than I had imagined I would after my reading session. I used to get a bit hot under the collar sometimes during the student protests, but the anger I felt rising in me now was something quite different. It was mixed with despair, sadness, impotence, and disbelief.

When I arrived gasping for breath at Nippon, I was afraid Takahashi-san would somehow know from looking at me what I had been up to. I avoided his gaze for the first few minutes, unnecessarily, I must say. He was prepping for dinner, and as soon as I arrived, he asked if I could assist Goto-san, fetch ingredients from the pantry, chop vegetables. He was cheerful that evening and joked around with me, Goto-san, and Hitomi. For example, he pretended to speak to the fish he was preparing, stuck its head between his fingers and made its mouth move so the plump mackerel seemed to be talking back. Normally I would have found it hilarious to watch Takahashi-san speak Japanese to a fish and hear the fish reply rather rudely in English: "I can't understand a word you say. Don't you know how to talk properly?" Yet I had to force myself to smile because I couldn't push aside the images I had seen in the library, couldn't reconcile them with his and Miko's past life in that city and with the jovial mood in the kitchen. I felt dazed and oddly numb. If Takahashi-san noticed, he didn't say anything but continued to play around, perhaps to try to cheer me up. In the end it worked, because as the evening went on, I relaxed and, for a while at least, was able to stop thinking about my trip to the library.

As usual, Goto-san and Hitomi left before I did, and Takahashi-san sat at the little desk from where he ran the restaurant. It was in a tiny nook off the kitchen, with a high window that overlooked the backyard. He wasn't interested in the management side of the business, but even so, he taught me the importance of not letting anything slide. He paid his bills in good time, kept precise accounts, made sure the grocery orders were up to date and that we always had the ingredients and utensils we needed. He also used to jot things down in a notebook he kept on the shelf above his desk next to his other books, which were all in Japanese. I didn't know what he wrote in his notebook, although I imagined some of it related to the business, as I frequently heard him say "I must write that down," or words to that effect. Occasionally it was in relation to the customers—their names, birthdays, favorite food. Other times he jotted down new words or expressions he wanted to remember; that was mainly on weekends, when Steve was working, because he didn't learn much English from Goto-san.

I was preparing to go home that evening when he called out to me: "Kristófer-san," he said, "I want to show you something."

I put down my apron and poked my head into the nook, where he was waiting for me with his notebook open.

"Do you know what a haiku is?"

I shook my head.

He explained. "Do you have anything like that in Icelandic?"

Although it was quite different, I thought the quatrain might be closest. "But there are four lines in every stanza," I said.

"Kristófer-san, it's the most difficult thing to express your thoughts in few words."

I nodded.

"I have just composed a haiku about the fish. I think he merited it."

He passed me the notebook.

It seems that the fish
has no time for Japanese
here in our kitchen.

We both smiled, and after holding his hand out for the notebook, he closed it. "It's good to laugh sometimes, Kristófer-san. It lifts the spirits."

I agreed, turning slightly red at the same time, because now I knew he had noticed my low mood. I was on the verge of giving some explanation, saying I was under the weather, feeling winded, but I let it rest.

"When I was young," he went on, "I worked my way through school at a small restaurant in my hometown. In the kitchen we kept a pot for haikus. We would write them down on a slip of paper which we folded and placed in the pot. Whenever one of us walked past it, we would reach inside and read the others' poems. There weren't many of us, so we all knew each other's handwriting. Sometimes we would get somebody to write down our haikus for us, just for fun or so that familiarity didn't cloud people's judgment. You see, sometimes it was desirable. To remain anonymous.

"I've been thinking about whether I should have a pot like that here in the kitchen," he went on. "Or maybe in reception. I've been giving it a lot of thought lately." He looked at me, awaiting a response.

I told him I thought it was a good idea. "I for one would read them."

He reached for a book on the shelf above his desk and handed it to me. *Traditional Japanese Haikus*, it said on the cover, above the translator's name.

"I bought this when I first started trying to compose in English," he said. "It's difficult for me, Kristófer-san. As difficult as it is for a fish to speak Japanese."

I turned the book over and read the back, then was going to hand it back to him.

"You can keep it. I doubt Steve will compose much for the pot. Goto-san and Hitomi neither. Not in English, anyway."

I thanked him, though I felt bound to point out I was no poet.

"So we have something in common," he said, and smiled.

Then he rose to his feet and I fetched my coat. Soon afterward we walked outside together and said goodbye.

I am standing down by the Thames after a pleasant morning stroll. I started off at the university campus, but everything was closed and there wasn't much to see, so I thought it best to go somewhere else. I didn't feel exactly melancholy, but after that wild-goose chase and my visit to Nippon—or should I say the tattoo parlor—I decided it was a waste of time going to any more of my old haunts. I hadn't really planned to visit my alma mater, so perhaps "wild-goose chase" is a slight exaggeration, but the place was so deserted I thought it sensible to leave before the emptiness got to me. I wandered off without a plan and soon found myself in Leicester Square and then in St. James's Park. Despite there being more ducks than people, I enjoyed a stroll along the pathways and had a good rest on a bench, where I was able to watch the Household Cavalry perform their duties. Some of the sentries stood erect and completely still, while others led statuesque horses by the reins around the gravel pitch and were so perfectly in step with one another that they might have been counting under their breath. The ceremony itself is rather meaningless, yet I found it heartening to watch, for it felt good to know that not everything has been turned upside down.

Before leaving the hotel, I checked Facebook and saw there was a message waiting for me from Miko. Naturally I jumped, needlessly, as it turned out, since she was simply apologizing for having still not given me the promised explanation. She didn't say much except that her symptoms had worsened, she felt weak and nauseated, was sleeping a lot, and couldn't concentrate on anything. I replied immediately, told her not to worry about me, and almost said something to her about this journey I have embarked upon. Luckily I thought better of it, because this morning the receptionist told me flights are being canceled left and right, including those to Japan, although my airline insists the flight this evening is on schedule. But that could change, he warned, and cited the example of two groups of guests whose flights were canceled this morning just as they were preparing to leave for the airport. "Practically without warning," he explained, adding that they were lucky the hotel was half empty, as he was able to offer them ongoing accommodations.

Miko made light of her illness and I felt I could actually hear her voice when she said she was being "an embarrassing wreck." I smiled to myself but then grew concerned because I know she doesn't complain easily.

But here I am now, standing by the river, and have been reflecting a little about something that shows how mysterious the workings of the human mind can be. You see, the idea occurred to me somewhere between St. James's Park and Westminster Bridge that perhaps Naruki and Miko did end up together. It's probably all in my mind and simply the sign of an overactive imagination, and yet as I was looking at the London Eye, the giant Ferris wheel on the far side of the river, I suddenly became convinced that Naruki's surname was Nakamura.

Obviously the Ferris wheel has nothing to do with Naruki, his name or surname, so I don't know why I thought of him at this particular moment. I had first noticed the wheel while I was watching the Household Cavalry, the top of it being visible above the Horse Guards building. I did have the impression it was moving more slowly than usual, although it was difficult to tell from that distance. Only when I reached the river, where there were no buildings to obscure the gigantic wheel, did I realize that it had simply ground to a halt.

By then my mind had become occupied with Naruki, and I am still thinking about him as I lean over the sturdy iron guardrail down here by the riverbank watching the Thames flow past. I am remembering the day he came to Nippon and the repercussions of his visit.

It was on Tuesday after lunch, around half past three. I had left at a quarter past but forgotten my wallet and had to go back. When I opened the door, Takahashi-san and Naruki were sitting alone in the dining room. They paid no attention to me, or maybe they just didn't notice me, as I tried to be discreet. Takahashi-san was doing all the talking; the young man replied in monosyllables. They were speaking in Japanese, so I couldn't understand a word.

At first I was nervous that Naruki had come to speak to Takahashi-san about his relationship with Miko, even to ask for her hand in marriage, which I understood was the custom in Japan. I had reached the kitchen by then and found my wallet, but instead of leaving, I stood motionless by the door and listened, trying to deduce from their voices what was going on between them.

Hitomi had gone out after lunch and Goto-san was taking a nap in the pantry. His low snores mingled with the murmur of the conversation in the dining room but didn't prevent me from coming to the swift conclusion that Naruki was having a hard time.

Not that Takahashi-san was aggressive in any way, he seemed rather to be advising the young man and confiding in him at the same time. On the few occasions when Naruki managed to utter a whole sentence, I had the impression he was clutching at straws, possibly even apologizing; in any case, he sounded dispirited.

Hearing them rise to their feet, I sneaked into the backyard and waited there for ten minutes. By then Takahashi-san was at his desk, apparently lost in thought. I was careful not to disturb him as I hurriedly left.

When Miko came to work on Friday afternoon, I was on edge after the meeting between Naruki and Takahashi-san and her revelation about Hiroshima. I wondered whether she might say something more about their past. I found it unlikely. We hadn't spoken since her lunch shift was over on Sunday.

She arrived early. I was cleaning up in the kitchen and didn't hear her come in. We had been busy at lunchtime and even busier at breakfast, when it was just Takahashi-san and me, as always. To my surprise, he had asked me to scale and grill the salmon that morning and then shown me how to pickle some vegetables. After that it was a bit difficult to return to my dishwashing duty when Goto-san arrived at midday. But I was grateful to Takahashi-san and had no reason to complain.

I didn't know how long she had been standing behind me before I finally noticed her. She was leaning against the wall, arms folded, and although it seemed she had been watching me wiping and tidying, her face was oddly blank, as if she had just been gazing at the sky or at a bird flying past.

Takahashi-san was at his desk in the nook with his back turned and hadn't noticed her either, not until she started talking.

"You're becoming like a Japanese person, Kristófer." Her voice had a strange tone. I wasn't sure how to respond. "Everything spick-and-span, everything in order . . . even your gestures."

Takahashi-san stopped what he was doing and looked over

his shoulder, contemplating us briefly before turning back to his desk, apparently waiting for whatever would come next.

"I'm just tidying up," I managed to say.

"You're even starting to look like Takahashi-san and Goto-san," she said.

I was at a loss for an answer. I wasn't sure if she was pulling my leg or criticizing me, accusing me of being a phony, of trying to be like her father, maybe to ingratiate myself with him. In any event, before I could open my mouth, she went on: "Do you have a girlfriend?"

I was not sure if I succeeded in concealing my embarrassment. "No."

"Have you ever had a girlfriend?"

"Yes."

"Did you talk much with her father?"

"Stop it, Miko." Takahashi-san was sitting still, looking straight ahead; he didn't raise his voice. She ignored him and waited for me to reply.

"I never met him."

"What? You mean you and he didn't discuss your relationship with his daughter?"

"No," I said, and then in the silence that ensued, I declared: "It wasn't serious."

Even as I spoke, I could see from her expression that I had made a blunder. My intention for this explanation had simply been to end the conversation she had dragged me into, but that didn't happen.

"Oh," she said. "It wasn't serious . . ."

"No," I repeated.

"What exactly do you mean? What makes a relationship serious?"

I shot Takahashi-san a sidelong glance but could see only his neck and shoulders. He was sitting very still.

"Neither of us had any expectations," I was able to stammer.

"So that's what makes a relationship serious," she said. "Expectations . . ."

I saw no point in replying, and anyway, she carried straight on: "Nothing else . . . Not whether you . . ."

At this point Takahashi-san sprang to his feet. I flinched, but Miko seemed to be expecting it and stood firm. He didn't say a word, and they just stared at each other amid a silence so deafening it made my ears ring.

When at last Takahashi-san spoke, he addressed me. "My apologies, Kristófer-san. You must be wanting to leave."

I realized I was still clasping the tea towel, so I set it down before going to fetch my coat. When I glanced at them on my way out, they were standing in the same position as before, yet somehow they both seemed smaller. Their heads were lowered, their shoulders slumped, and in place of the anger I had sensed a moment ago, a strange sadness enveloped both of them.

I don't understand how I could have let Mundi upset me like this. Needless to say, this thing with Baldur is complete nonsense, at best a misunderstanding or else an exaggeration, although sadly, I can't help suspecting Mundi of some darker motive. He thrives on making a mountain out of a molehill, takes pleasure in discovering and exploiting weaknesses; he calls it teasing, but "nastiness" is probably a better word. He has always been like that. But this is crossing a line, and it's hardly surprising if I object to being accused of mistreating my closest staff member.

Baldur was the first one I told I was going to call it a day. As I said, it happened very fast, with the virus coming out of nowhere, as it did. He was taken aback but after we had discussed my decision, he realized that although it was made in haste, I didn't have much of a choice.

Actually I am going to make a point of remembering that conversation, even if it's only to rid myself of the anguish Mundi's message has caused me.

It was on a Tuesday morning, shortly before ten o'clock. I had returned from the doctor, so I may have been a bit distracted when I walked through the door. At least, he asked me if everything was okay when I entered the kitchen, where he was prepping for the day even though business was already slow. I suggested he take a short break from work and we sat in the dining room, by the west-facing wall where you can see all the way down the street to Austurvöllur Square.

I saw no need to tell him where I had just been. Instead, I evoked the old days, as my memories were beginning to haunt me. "It was Bjarni Jónsson who had the steakhouse here in the old days," I said.

Baldur said he remembered it.

"But his steaks weren't any good, and the walls were very dark."

He nodded, because admittedly I had spoken about this before.

"I ate at his restaurant once," I said, "only I wasn't thinking then about how to make the place more attractive. Maybe I was too busy trying to find some flavor in the steak!"

Baldur smiled.

"You never got to know Bjarni, did you?"

"No."

"He was a nice enough fellow. But he knew nothing about food. For years he ran a hamburger joint down by the harbor, but this place was supposed to put him on the map. He took it badly when things didn't work out."

Baldur and I had often talked about the difference between a restaurant that enjoyed brief popularity and then foundered, and one that carved a niche, retained a loyal customer base while attracting new patrons, stood the test of time, adapted to new trends without changing its character. We invariably came to the conclusion that the biggest difference was in the food itself, the raw ingredients, the way they were handled, simple presentation, resourcefulness, creativity, and lack of pretension. As well as excellent service, a warm atmosphere, and reasonable prices.

So he wasn't surprised when I said that Bjarni's ignorance about food came back to haunt him, that he was more interested in his jukebox, proudly displayed beside the bar, and would tell the story of how he had brought it over from the States to anyone willing to listen.

"So when I came here with the real estate agent, I knew immediately this was where I wanted to be," I said. "Before we even crossed the threshold, I had decided not only to rent the place but also what changes I wanted to make. I instantly felt at home."

Baldur said he had felt the same way. "I had just been for an interview at Hotel Holt," he said. "But then I bumped into Ásberg in the mall and he told me you were hiring. The truth is, I always intended to take the job at Hotel Holt if they offered it to me. This was just a backup."

I told him I had forgotten that.

"I don't think I ever told you," he said, and smiled. "And then I did get the job at Hotel Holt and had to choose."

"I hope you don't regret coming here," I said.

"I never have. At Hotel Holt I only ever would have been a head chef."

I assumed Baldur was referring to the fact that over the years I have consulted him about most things relating to the management of Torg, including advertising and website design, pricing, and, without exception, hiring. When I had the place repainted the year before last, I even asked his opinion about the color. We agreed it should be another pale shade but slightly warmer. So he has certainly learned a lot more than he would have at Hotel Holt.

"But this is it for me," I went on. "For weeks if not months there will be no guests, and we obviously can't survive on take-aways and deliveries. Maybe for me this is just a reminder that enough is enough."

Baldur said he wasn't entirely surprised, because even before the pandemic I had made a few references to my retirement, spoken about not getting any younger and things like that. "How long is left on the lease?" he asked.

"Fourteen months," I said.

"Has Frissi said anything about not renewing if it came to that?" he asked.

"Frissi? No, he wants us to stay. That's not why I am retiring now," I added.

Baldur said things wouldn't be the same without me. "You've done so much for the restaurant business here in Reykjavík," he said.

"And now it's your turn to take over. You young people. You're far more talented than I was at your age."

"Thanks," he said. "Thanks for everything, Kristófer."

Just then the door opened and Steinunn walked in.

"We'll finish this later," I said, "but I think you'll be pleased."

Baldur isn't usually formal, but he shook my hand and thanked me once more for having faith in him, as he put it.

We didn't have the chance to speak again until two days ago, because I had to go over the accounts and bank statements first to see how long I could afford to carry on paying him. I called him early in the morning because I didn't want to keep him guessing, and besides, I thought I was the bearer of good tidings.

The conversation was brief, and I suspect I might have gotten him out of bed. I told him I intended to pay his salary in full until the end of the year. He kept saying "What?" as if he didn't understand, so I told him again. This gave him plenty of time, I explained, to look around, decide what to do next.

"And to spend time with your family," I added. "My namesake will enjoy that."

I haven't heard from him since. But I made the transfer into his account before I left, so he won't need to worry about money in the near term.

I believed I treated him well, I believed I acted for the best. But now, undoubtedly without any justification, Mundi has destroyed the peace of mind that paying Baldur gave me and caused me to no longer feel sure about anything.

I am wondering whether I ought to speak to Baldur directly. This isn't the ideal moment, as I am about to reach the airport and all indications are that my flight will leave at seven. But I have some time to think about it, and if it seems like the right thing to do, I can call him later. Until then, I will do my best to forget Mundi's messages.

We are in the air. The sky is clear as I watch the lights of the city disappear and those in cities east of it get closer. But then a few wispy clouds appear, tinged by the sun's last rays, and the lights vanish.

I'm sitting by the window and there is nobody in the seats next to me, as the plane is half empty. The majority of the passengers are Japanese people returning home; I am in a minority. Not that it bothered me, but when we assembled at the departure gate, I got a few strange looks, and then a young man wearing a face mask asked me why I was going to Tokyo. He was Japanese and I had a little difficulty understanding him because of his mask, but I found his curiosity inoffensive, so I explained that I was visiting friends. I don't know why I find it so hard to talk about my friend in singular, but that's the way it is. Later I realized it would have been polite of me to ask the reason for his trip, but unfortunately it didn't occur to me.

But now all is quiet and the plane is tracing a slow arc on the screen in front of me, where it will fly over Sweden and Finland before turning north over Russia and finally south to the Pacific Ocean. It's a long way, but I have plenty to occupy my mind, so it doesn't matter that I didn't bring any reading material other than the anthology of traditional Japanese poetry.

I finally sent Miko a message telling her I am on my way. I waited until it was almost time to embark, since I didn't want to risk receiving a reply before I boarded the plane. I got a little worried because I couldn't get an Internet connection by the departure gate, but then the young man with the face mask suggested I move off to the side, as that usually worked for him. He was right—there was an excellent connection a short distance away—and I put on my glasses, quickly typed my message, and pressed send, and even more quickly slipped my phone back in my pocket, even though she was probably fast asleep, as it was the middle of the night in Japan.

My mind goes back to the day Takahashi-san apologized to me. I can see the expression on his and Miko's faces when I put down the tea towel and grabbed my coat, as well as when I returned at about five o'clock. It is Miko's laughter that first comes to mind because it greeted me the instant I opened the door. I remember stopping in my tracks, for it seemed so incompatible with the unhappy atmosphere permeating the premises when I'd left two hours earlier.

She was joking around with Hitomi, who was working that evening because one of their regulars had booked the restaurant for his birthday. We were expecting more guests than there were seats and had therefore created a buffet menu—*gyoza*, edamame, *tsukune* with sweet soy sauce, *yakitori* skewers, *teba shio*, and probably a few other finger foods I can no longer remember.

The two of them were laughing heartily. I hung up my coat in the closet, changed my shoes, and put my apron on. I was nervous about meeting Takahashi-san, but I needn't have worried, as he also behaved as if nothing had happened.

"Ah, Kristófer-san, we need more scallions."

The evening was a festive one. I stole furtive glances at Miko as she waited on and chatted with the guests, weaving deftly between them, serving them food, refilling their glasses. Maybe it was my imagination, but I thought she hadn't quite managed to erase all traces of her earlier exchange with her father, detecting beneath her smile a glimpse of that strange melancholy I had witnessed before. It seemed to make her smile more beautiful and genuine, more meaningful. I could have continued watching her forever.

I was so entranced that I didn't manage to look away when she noticed me. She was standing in the dining room holding a bowl of edamame, and I was in the kitchen doorway. We looked into each other's eyes. I once again had the feeling she could see inside me.

The party lasted until after midnight. Having completed his chores, Takahashi-san mingled with the birthday boy and his guests. He drank sake and seemed happy. Hitomi and Steve went home, and I cleared up.

I was finishing when Miko came into the kitchen. She said nothing, just walked up to me and placed her hand on my cheek. She caressed me gently, pausing until at last she drew her hand away. Neither of us said a word.

That night I went to sleep with her palm on my cheek. I awoke with it the next day, but by then I was filled with a strange fear, bordering on foreboding. I became aware of it the instant I opened my eyes; it was as if it emanated from a dream I had just forgotten. I didn't know then what it was that I was afraid of, but later, when everything was over and I looked back on that day and the days that followed, I couldn't help wondering if I had already begun to sense the ending.

The day after the birthday party, a pot appeared on the bar with a slip of folded paper in it. I arrived early and noticed the pot immediately but didn't take out the slip of paper, although I thought I knew what it was. It was an old ceramic pot, blue and white with a flower design and butterflies among the petals. When I mentioned it to Takahashi-san, he feigned surprise, then asked if I had read what was on the slip of paper. I put my apron on and went back out to the bar.

Of course, it was a haiku, written in black ink on white paper. Takahashi-san had a distinctive scrawl which showed he was more accustomed to writing in Japanese than in English. But it was easy to read and pleasing to the eye in its simplicity, perfectly suited to a haiku.

The birthday party
over, the same food once more
on every table.

I had been browsing through the book on Japanese poetry and was becoming quite familiar with the haiku, the subtle nuances, the necessity of hinting at things rather than spelling them out, the writer's trust in the reader to be able to read between the lines. In this one I understood that the food served the day before was no longer available but also sensed something about transience, everyday continuity, interrupted fleetingly by changes that are forgotten or perhaps live only in memory.

But I didn't say any of that to Takahashi when he asked me what exactly was on the slip of paper. I simply replied: "Apparently we have the same old menu again."

The happy bantering came as a timely release, since I needed to rid myself of the apprehension that had been plaguing me all morning. More than once I had caught myself touching my cheek where Miko had caressed me, as if to try to comprehend the meaning of her gesture. I thought I had the evening before, when she walked up to me and stretched out her hand, when she looked into my eyes. But now I wasn't so sure, as doubt had reared its head and derailed my thoughts.

I longed for her to arrive and yet dreaded it at the same time. When at last she showed up with a few minutes to spare before the lunch shift, I was none the wiser, although she greeted me with a smile and whispered: "I'm late. Has Dad said anything?"

No, he hadn't mentioned his daughter but had been in a talkative mood, had spoken about the birthday party, haikus, and the mackerel he wasn't happy with that day. Steve had had one too many the night before, was off color and a bit sluggish, so Takahashi-san let me help prep for lunch. I coated the chicken breasts in flour, egg batter, and breadcrumbs, fried them, and cut them into strips. This was an unexpected privilege, as Takahashi-san was very fastidious when it came to *katsu* dishes and would get annoyed if the pork or chicken wasn't cooked exactly right. The oil couldn't be too cold or too hot, the panko breadcrumbs had to cover the whole breast and not crumble when fried, the color should be golden brown but not too dark and never burned. Obviously the chicken couldn't be allowed to dry out, so timing was essential, although the clock was only in your head. This was easier said than done, and I had witnessed Takahashi-san gasp when Steve took his eye off the ball, although he generally kept quiet and instead discreetly got rid of the morsels that didn't look right.

I couldn't help feeling a flash of pride after lunch when Takahashi-san complimented me. He especially remarked that he hadn't needed to remind me to cut the meat at an angle rather than straight across, a technique called *sogigiri*, often used to slice fish or vegetables into bite-size chunks. Maybe it was his praise that gave me the courage to mention something I had been mulling over for the past few days. I had planned to several times but always gotten cold feet at the last minute. Specifically, I wanted to know if I was capable of cooking a whole meal on my own. Breakfast was the obvious choice, as I had the advantage of having worked alongside Takahashi-san so many mornings and knew his recipes backward and forward, in theory, at least. In addition, my little experiment would be easy enough to set up, since so far Takahashi-san had resisted the pressure from some of his regular customers to open for breakfast more often.

To cut a long story short, he embraced my idea. I had rehearsed a speech aimed at reassuring him that I would clear away every sign of my experiment before he arrived in the morning and, in addition, use the ingredients sparingly and pay for them out of my own pocket. My speech was unnecessary, however, as he wouldn't hear of me paying for anything. He smiled and then asked if I had a particular day in mind; my enthusiasm seemed to please him.

"Tuesday," I said, "if that's suitable." He told me Tuesday was fine and reminded me to ask him for the keys the day before.

We were alone when we had that conversation, as I had taken the opportunity when Steve and Miko left for their midday break. Which is why I was surprised in the evening, after we had closed and finished clearing away, when Miko mentioned this scheme of mine. I had gone to the backyard to kick up my feet and have a beer before heading home, as it was warm outside and I was in no hurry to leave while she was still there. She pushed open the door and asked me as she stepped outside: "What exactly are you planning to cook?"

I was surprised but managed nonetheless to answer her without trouble.

"And who is going to judge your performance?"

I said I would have to be my own judge, as I had told Takahashi-san that I wasn't inviting anybody.

"You can cook for me . . ."

I felt a surge of euphoria run through my veins and took a while to respond.

"If you want . . ."

It was dusky out in the yard with only the kitchen lights on, and yet I could see, or maybe sense, a hesitancy in her which I had never witnessed before. As if she wasn't sure I would accept her proposal and was possibly even expecting to be disappointed. What surprised me most was that she should fear being disappointed.

"Yes," I said at last, "but you mustn't judge me too harshly."

"You're afraid I will?"

"Of course."

She drew closer to me. For a moment I thought she might be going to place her hand on my cheek like the night before. I instinctively sat up, but she stopped a few feet away and looked at me in the semi-darkness. A soft light fell on her cheek.

"I can be a harsh judge."

"I am sure you can."

"But I can also be indulgent . . . with people I'm fond of."

I was about to stand up and go toward her, for I longed to embrace her. But then she added in her customary mocking voice: "Provided I think they deserve it."

Then she turned on her heel and, before I knew it, had vanished into the kitchen.

Although I haven't cooked a Japanese breakfast since I lived in London fifty years ago, I feel confident that I would acquit myself well enough if put to the test. Not because I consider myself a particularly talented cook; quite the contrary. But I think I can still rely on my general experience and, even more importantly, on my memory of the time I cooked for Miko, which I expect will be one of the very last things erased from my brain if indeed the doctor's diagnosis is correct.

The cooking itself isn't very complicated. The challenge for the chef is precision in timekeeping because all the dishes must be served at the same time. Takahashi-san maintained that attitude was more important than technique, and this applied equally to breakfast, lunch, or dinner.

He used to say that breakfast resembles the first line of a haiku, it shows the way. Lunch is the second line and carries the momentum. The third line, then, is dinner, as it brings everything to a close.

Naturally I intended to practice as much as I could before Miko came to critique my performance, but now I wished I had chosen Thursday instead of Tuesday. I had only two days to get ready, and all of a sudden I felt totally unprepared.

I made no mention of Miko to Takahashi-san when I asked if I could have the keys sooner than intended so that I could start practicing. Not that I meant to deceive him, but he didn't ask, and so I said nothing.

He took the keys from his desk drawer and handed them to me. "Keep them," he said. "They may come in handy one day if you arrive for the breakfast shift before me."

I slept hardly a wink on Saturday night, and on Sunday morning I was in the kitchen by six o'clock. There I worked nonstop until Takahashi-san arrived at nine: boiling the seaweed and dried tuna flakes for the miso soup, pickling the vegetables, steaming the rice, dicing tofu. I cured two salmon fillets in salt and put them in the fridge for the following day, then grilled a fresh piece with a splash of vinegar. As I said, the cookery is comparatively simple, but as anyone who eats Japanese food knows, no two miso soups are the same, and steamed rice can be both good and bad.

Shortly after eight o'clock I had finished preparing the meal. At first I was satisfied with how it turned out, but then a succession of criticisms kept popping into my head—the soup was too bland, the salmon overgrilled, the rice too sticky. The vegetables not pickled enough. The tofu soggy.

By the time Takahashi-san arrived, I had finished clearing everything away. He cast his eye over the kitchen and I could see he was content, as there was no trace of my having worked there, aside from the lingering aromas.

The next morning I repeated the exercise, stopping off at five to buy salmon at our fishmonger's, arriving an hour later in the kitchen. I managed to prepare two breakfasts and felt more satisfied than the day before, especially with the first one. Yet I knew I could do better, though I couldn't quite figure out what was missing.

And then, Monday lunchtime, it occurred to me I should add some clams to the soup. I had seen Takahashi-san do it once. Clams were expensive and not always available, but I needed only a few, and I had seen them at the fishmonger's that morning, baby clams which he told me he sold to several restaurants, including the new Japanese place, Akiko, near Saint Paul's Cathedral.

I slept very little on Monday night, if at all. Even so, I was wide awake when I set off for Nippon in the early-morning gloom. A sliver of dawn was visible in the east, where the sky was beginning to brighten in contrast with a bank of dark but harmless-looking clouds. The air was still and rather mild, a sign of settled weather in the coming days.

I listened to my footsteps echo in the silence as I switched on the lights, changed my clothes, lit the stove, took out knives and pincers, chopping boards, trays, pots and pans. I fetched out of the fridge the broth I'd prepared the previous day, checked the salmon I had cured overnight, sampled the plums I had pickled and stored in a jar, and the chopped ginger I had pickled in plum brine a week ago when I was assisting Takahashi-san.

Time went by quickly. Six o'clock, seven. The early-morning light flowed through the windows and illuminated the dining room, where I stood wondering where best to have Miko sit. Finally I chose a table in the back because I had heard her recommend it a few times to customers she liked.

She arrived at exactly half past seven, as we had discussed. She was dressed in jeans and a red turtleneck sweater I hadn't seen her wear before. She had tied her hair up in a bun and wore a pair of tiny earrings.

"Do you need any help?"

"No," I said, and asked her to take a seat at the table I had selected.

"Here?"

"Yes."

"Which side?"

"You choose."

"In that case, I'll sit facing the kitchen so I can see you come out."

She sat down. I went into the kitchen to add the finishing touches to her breakfast. I put the clams I had already washed in the simmering miso soup, grilled the salmon, placed a bowl of steamed rice on the tray next to the vegetables I had arranged on a square plate with a picture of a tiny smiling Buddha. The salmon and the miso soup were ready at the same time, and having put them on the tray, I took it out and set it on the table in front of her. I had the impression she hadn't moved while I was in the kitchen, but she looked up as soon as I emerged holding the tray and watched me as I crossed the floor and after I had set the tray down. I noticed her eyes were on me and not the tray. Then she smiled, looked down, and studied the dishes.

"I'll fetch some tea," I said.

We all had our own mugs which we kept on a shelf in the kitchen. Mine was rather plain—white with a Leeds United crest on the back and the front, whereas Miko, like her father, Hitomi, and Goto-san, all had traditional Japanese ceramic mugs without a handle.

I poured some green tea into her mug and carried it over to her. She had made a start on the salmon, eaten two clams from the soup, and was taking a piece of pickled plum in her chopsticks and placing it in her mouth. I stood still and waited for her to say something about my cooking. She ate slowly.

"What do you do when you aren't at work?"

Her question caught me unaware. "What do I do?"

"Yes, when you aren't here."

"I read, listen to music, watch football, meet my friends . . ."

"The ones who were with you at the bookshop?"

"Yes, for example."

"Are they fun?"

"They're okay."

"Do you miss university?"

"No."

She looked me in the eye and then, apparently satisfied by what she saw, said, "I believe you." She picked up a morsel of salmon with her chopsticks. She chewed slowly. "Were you a bad student?"

"No, I was actually a good student."

"Hm."

"You don't believe me?"

"Yes, I believe you. Do you miss Iceland?"

I wasn't sure how to respond, because I missed nothing when I was in her company. "No," I said at last. "Do you miss Japan?"

"I was two when we left, and I haven't been back since."

I felt my question was foolish, even though her reply hadn't insinuated that.

"There's no need to be embarrassed," she said. "You couldn't have known."

She still hadn't said anything about the food. I was beginning to get worried. And yet she was eating: fished out another clam, raised the bowl of miso to her lips, continued to munch on the pickles, added some soy sauce to her rice.

"What was your girlfriend's name?"

I gave a start.

"The one you told Takahashi-san and me about the other day."

"Hildur," I said.

"Is she in Iceland?"

"Yes."

"At university?"

"Yes."

"Did you sleep together?"

For some reason my embarrassment had evaporated. "Yes," I replied.

"What was it like?"

"I'm sorry?"

"Was it good?"

I managed to produce a stammering "yes."

"And yet it wasn't serious?"

"No, it wasn't."

"So you didn't love her?"

I had to pause, for I didn't know how to explain to her that before I met her, I had no idea what love was.

"I thought so at the time," I said.

"But?"

"I was fond of her."

"There's a difference, isn't there?"

I nodded.

"I was fond of Naruki," she said.

She put down her chopsticks and sat very still. I didn't move either, afraid to break the silence with something I might regret.

"Why did you apply for the job here?" she asked.

I knew I couldn't avoid telling her the truth. "Because of you."

"When we met in the doorway?"

"Yes."

"When you were going out and I was coming in?"

"Yes."

"I told my dad not to hire you."

"Why?"

"So he would hire you."

She rose slowly to her feet. I took two steps forward, covering the distance that separated us.

I found her lips as I embraced her, then clasped her in my arms as if wanting to make sure I would never lose her.

Irasshaimase! Irasshaimase!

We have landed and are met by three airport attendants when we disembark, two men and a woman who bow as they greet us. They are all wearing face masks, as are the majority of passengers. I forgot to buy any before I left London, as they are difficult to find, but one of the flight attendants came to my rescue, so I am equipped, temporarily, at least.

There aren't many people at the airport, so it doesn't take long to get through. Everywhere I receive a warm welcome, especially at passport control, where they tell me they don't see many Icelandic visitors.

This is the first time I have visited Japan. I was often on the verge of booking a flight here, but I always changed my mind. Naturally, I could have come without looking for Miko, simply traveled, visited the temples at Kyoto and Nara, the emperor's palace in Tokyo, sampled the nightlife in Shinjuku. Or even gone to Hokkaido in the north, to the port areas of Hakodate or Otaru, which are famous for their seafood, in particular sea urchins. I could have gone hiking in the mountains around Koyasan, followed the old pilgrims' route and steered clear of Hiroshima, overcome the temptation to visit that part of the country. And yet I held back, knowing I wouldn't be able to control myself, even if Inga was with me.

Not that I knew where Miko and Takahashi-san lived. I had no idea. I wasn't sure they were in Japan; they could just as well have moved somewhere else. And yet it was the most obvious choice, there or to some of the English towns where I had gone looking after they disappeared.

I continued to collect books, articles, anything and everything relating to Japan after I moved back to Iceland. In fact, I gained a reputation as something of an authority on the country and its people. Frankly, this was hardly warranted, as I was only slightly better informed than the average person. I should also mention that I didn't go around boasting about it; rather, it was Inga who would bring up the subject. She did so in such a way that no one suspected she had a problem with it. But I knew the truth. I knew she hated it, which was why when my anthology of haikus went missing from my bedside table, I packed most of my books and videotapes into boxes, films by well-known directors such as Kurosawa and Ozu, Shōhei Imamura and Kaneto Shindo, among them *Children of Hiroshima*. I had also collected documentaries on a wide range of subjects: travelogues, programs on Japanese history, cuisine, birdlife, Buddhism, pottery, to name a few. Some of them were in Japanese without subtitles, but I always learned something from watching them.

I took some of the books and videotapes to Torg and kept them in a cupboard in my little office. I also bought a portable TV with a built-in VCR which sat on top of the filing cabinet, where I could watch it from my swivel chair if I turned around.

When Inga passed away, I brought one of the boxes up from

the basement and reinstalled the books in the living room where they had been originally. Not immediately, I should say, but little by little. First one book, then another, the occasional film I felt like watching again. And then one box after another. I don't think I threw anything out even when I finally sold our terraced house and moved to the city center.

I am holding one of those books now. *Japanese for Beginners*, which, although it's a bit out of date, has proved useful on my taxi ride from the airport, as the driver speaks no English. But he was quick to respond to my efforts, and we've agreed the weather is not too bad even if the sun isn't shining. He is a friendly fellow who drives with white gloves on, and although the fare is quite expensive, I don't regret permitting myself this luxury. I expect I could have made sense of the somewhat complicated train schedules, but why burden myself when it's only natural that I am tired after my journey.

The hotel I booked online two days ago is in the center of Tokyo, nice and clean, if the pictures on the website are anything to go by. They gave me a good deal because here, as everywhere, tourists are dwindling. The taxi driver confirmed this. He said he has half as many fares. "*Gojupasento*," he said, raising his right hand, fingers splayed. "*Goju*."

The doorman who receives me when we arrive at the hotel is wearing a face mask and surgical gloves. He sprays the bags with sanitizer after taking them out of the trunk and then wipes them thoroughly with a cloth before placing them on his trolley. My temperature is taken at the entrance before I am allowed to approach the front desk. The receptionist, a young woman, hands me two sheets of printed paper in English explaining the hotel's safety protocol during the pandemic. The rooms are cleaned once a day instead of twice, she explains, but more in depth, which takes longer. The sauna is closed. They are not offering a buffet in the dining room. "Our apologies," she says, and bows.

"There's no need," I say.

I check the time when I get to my room. It's five-thirty in the afternoon. I am so used to having to calculate the time where Miko is located that I start to do so automatically. Then I give a start, as if it's only just dawned on me how close to her I am. Yes, I practically jump and open Facebook to check if she has replied to my message telling her that I am on my way to her. She hasn't yet. This makes me a little anxious, but then I tell myself that her not responding could be a positive sign, because honestly I am afraid she might oppose my trip. I remind myself of this as I stretch out on the bed and close my eyes, repeating to myself that no news is good news. I feel calm and reassured and, before I know it, drift off peacefully.

I imagined I might sleep for an hour at most, but when I finally come around, it's dark and I feel completely disoriented. It's ten o'clock at night. Fifteen after, to be exact. I can hear music playing, but I'm not sure whether it's coming from the corridor outside or from inside my head.

Foie gras, lumpfish roe, white asparagus . . . I go through my usual exercises, remember my ID card number, recite the menu in my head. But I keep hesitating and can only name every other starter, and even then I can't be sure that what I am remembering is actually correct. It's the white asparagus I have a particular problem with. I am certain of the lumpfish roe because I contacted the supplier myself and oversaw Baldur's experiments with lemon juice and chili. I can still taste the dish if I close my eyes.

I take a break, as there is no point in banging my head against the wall. I mustn't make too much out of this little hiccup; I am not properly awake. Outside, the city lights flicker: I have never seen so many of them. White, red, blue, and yellow everywhere. Orange. Violet. I am on the twentieth floor. I know this without having to look at the room key.

I open Facebook. Miko hasn't replied and I continue to see this as a good sign, although maybe my optimism is waning a little. I am still groggy and tired, however, so I resolve to ignore the doubts that have begun to assail me. They will evaporate once I have a shower and go outside, I am sure.

On the other hand, there is a message from Sonja. Three, to be exact, all sent within the last hour. She has developed an oddly telegraphic way of texting, a brusqueness that always makes me wonder what she may be keeping back.

The first message goes like this: "Did you forget his birth-day?"

The second: "March 20."

The third: "Tokyo?"

I instantly realize whose birthday she is referring to, because she reminded me about it last week and told me Villi was really looking forward to it.

"He's saving up for a new bicycle," she said.

"Oh."

"So it's best if you just give him some money."

At first glance this might seem like helpful information designed to spare me time and effort. And that's how I would probably see it if it weren't for the fact that I get the same call every year. The message always contains three instructions: "Don't forget Villi's birthday. Buy him a present. The present should be this or that." I admit that I do need reminding sometimes, as I have never been very good with birthdays. I don't write down the dates, although I probably ought to, so maybe I should be grateful to Sonja for nudging me. But quite frankly I am not, even though I am fond of young Villi and wouldn't wish to deprive him of a birthday present.

It's the way she goes about it that upsets me, her undisguised demandingness and bossiness bordering on the pathological. I should be used to it by now, I know, and yet somehow every year she manages to take me by surprise, riding roughshod over me, oblivious to my responses. Not that I tell her openly what I think about her overbearing behavior, but for heaven's sake, the woman is a trained social worker who ought to be more attuned to people's thoughts and feelings.

I feel refreshed after my shower, and although I am not all that hungry, I am going to try to find something to eat. The vibrant city draws me in, beckons me with its glittering lights and ceaseless throng as I step out onto the pavement. Even so, my head is filled with thoughts of Sonja, especially after the conversation I had with the young woman in reception as I was leaving.

I had stopped at the front desk to inquire about local restaurants. She was extremely helpful and took the opportunity to inform me that I need to vacate my room by noon tomorrow instead of at one o'clock, as stated on the website. Due to the change in cleaning regime, she explained, the management had decided to gain one hour from guests checking out and another from guests checking in, who now have to wait until three o'clock.

There was no question that she expected me to conform to the new rule without demur, and yet the way she made the request was so polite that anybody might think she was asking a favor of me which I was at liberty to refuse. She also thanked me profusely for my cooperation and understanding and invited me to partake of a complimentary two-course lunch in the frequent visitors' lounge on the second floor after I had vacated my room. Then she bowed, and I could see from her eyes that she was smiling behind her mask.

Sonja doesn't understand this kind of behavior, and I doubt

she could ever learn it. I probably shouldn't let her attitude affect me—or irritate me, as the doctor would put it—but I seem unable to control myself, at least when I am not feeling a hundred percent. And yet for the longest time I succeeded in ignoring this trait of hers and would simply nod when Inga made excuses for her, strange as they were. In particular the one about her difficult childhood, the toll that Inga and Orri's divorce had taken, and how, as a result, Sonja had needed to stand up for herself and develop a thick skin.

Inga said more or less the same thing on the few occasions when I brought up the subject of having children. She said she worried how Sonja might react, that a new baby might only make things worse. I found her choice of words unfortunate, but I let it pass. We hadn't been married long then, but maybe she already sensed we had enough on our hands with each other. At least that's what I sometimes imagine.

I am going to stop thinking about Sonja and her texts, which I have so far resisted answering, fortunately. Instead I intend to enjoy what remains of my evening in Tokyo after my unexpectedly long nap, and to prepare for the train journey south tomorrow. I am only about a fifteen-minute walk from the Shibuya neighborhood, where the receptionist recommended two restaurants. I can see the lights drawing closer; the sky is illuminated and changes color at regular intervals as if to a rhythmical command. The moon has risen in the north, and as I pause to look at it, I remember in a flash the thing I have been struggling with since I awoke from my nap, namely every item on the starter menu at Torg—beef tartare, salad and shellfish soup, besides the lumpfish roe, asparagus, and foie gras. I feel strangely relieved and quicken my step, for after all the thinking about food, I am suddenly very hungry.

The moonlight came in slantwise through the window and shone onto the wall next to the bed. There was nothing on it except a picture of Jesus Christ, approximately eight by twelve inches, which had been hung high up on the wall as if to ensure nothing obstructed his view.

She was lying in my arms, but now she sat up and stretched her hand out so the moon shone on her forearm. She held it there and then drew it back. "It's cold," she said.

"What?"

"The moonlight," she said. "It gives me goose bumps."

She seldom spent the night at my place, once a week at most. Instead we would meet whenever we could during the day. She was still living with her father in Hampstead, but I didn't know that before. At the restaurant she and her father seldom spoke about themselves.

"Feel." She stretched her hand out again.

I sat up and clasped her arm where the moon shone, then

moved my hand into the shadow. She looked at me, awaiting my verdict.

"Maybe," I said.

"Shut your eyes."

I did as she said. She guided my forefinger first to where the moon was and then to where it wasn't. "Surely you can feel it now."

"Yes, this is much cooler."

"Silly," she said, "that's the wrong place."

We lay down, I on my back. She kissed me, moved her hand beneath the sheets, and took hold of me. "Is this maybe the wrong place too?"

I had taken the room when I moved out of my dorm. It was on the top floor of a private residence in Kensington, a rather dilapidated house but clean inside. It suited me that the room was furnished and the rent reasonable. The owner, Mrs. Ellis, a widow of about seventy, lived on the ground floor and rented out the upstairs, which had three bedrooms and a bathroom. In the room next to me was a middle-aged man who worked at Harrods, and at the far end of the corridor next to the bathroom was a woman who worked in a library. I hardly saw them, as they were usually in bed by the time I got back from Nippon and left for work before I got up, except on the days when I helped Takahashi-san with breakfast; then I was up before them.

I hadn't had many guests until Miko started coming around. Mrs. Ellis had been clear when I moved in that she didn't tolerate noise or disturbance but that lodgers were welcome to have visitors and could receive them in the front room when she wasn't using it. Mrs. Ellis was extremely devout, as the picture of Jesus in my room suggested, and from time to time she would quote from the Bible, but not in a bothersome way. Downstairs she had several more pictures of the Savior, including one of him on the cross in the hallway. Once, when she asked me politely why I didn't shave off my beard and get a haircut, I had to stop myself from pointing out that the hirsute Savior in the pictures didn't look so very different from me.

I did my utmost to be discreet about Miko's visits, but it was inevitable that Mrs. Ellis occasionally caught a glimpse of her. She wasn't an inquisitive woman and never mentioned it to me, but I felt a bit uncomfortable with her knowing Miko was in my room on those quiet afternoons. As for Miko, it didn't bother her in the slightest.

"What difference does it make?" she said. "Has she ever come upstairs?"

Miko used to come over after her lectures or work on my days off. On my days at Nippon, I would sometimes rush home to meet her after my lunch shift, but less so in the summer, as it wasn't easy for her to get away from her job at the lab in the middle of the day. After we had been together, I always felt awkward when I met Takahashi-san back at the restaurant. I was afraid he could tell from looking at me what I had been up to, and I avoided his gaze. I also imagined he could smell Miko on me.

Whenever she stayed the night, we would sneak into the house late, after Mrs. Ellis and my fellow lodgers had gone to bed. It was more problematic for Miko to slip out unseen in the mornings, however quiet she was.

Miko told her father she was with her friend Elizabeth. She had been regularly sleeping over at her place since she started university, mostly if she was out late, going to a concert or a book reading, and couldn't be bothered to go home. Elizabeth was Scottish and, according to Miko, the soul of discretion; they were both studying psychology. I met her several times before Miko and Takahashi-san disappeared, and I liked her. She certainly wasn't responsible for Takahashi-san finding out about us.

"Why must Takahashi-san not know about us?"

"Why does he need to know about us?"

"I don't like sneaking behind his back."

"Neither do I."

"I thought he liked me."

"He does like you. He also liked Naruki."

"You're an adult . . ."

"I know what I am."

"I don't understand . . ."

She slid her hand beneath the sheets. "What don't you understand?"

I closed my eyes.

"Don't close them," she said. "Look into my eyes."

I did as she said. She moved her hand rhythmically up and down. When I closed my eyes again without meaning to, she whispered to me to keep them open. I felt she was looking deep inside me, studying every square inch of me, every last corner, as though searching for the source of my ecstasy, not only this fleeting ecstasy but also my love, to remember it, the way into it, to where it all originated.

Then she smiled her half smile and sat astride me, placed her hands flat against my chest, and began to rock back and forth, the moon shining on her raven hair.

Whenever we were together at Nippon, I found I could never predict how she would act toward me. Sometimes she ignored me, other times she teased me good-naturedly, still other times she praised me, though always with a hint of surprise in her voice, as if she was amazed I could set a table or cook ramen without messing it up. "Wow, they're exactly how they should be!"

Her behavior didn't bother me because I knew she was only trying to prevent our coworkers from finding out about us. On the other hand, it was often difficult for me to hide my feelings, and she would stare daggers at me at times, for example, if she caught me looking at her. I didn't do it on purpose; my lack of self-control was a continual source of worry to me.

The worst thing was having to go behind Takahashi-san's back. But Miko was adamant, and whenever I mentioned her father, she would snap at me or look sad, so I stopped. She gave me no explanation, and I knew better than to put pressure on her.

At the same time, I was on my best behavior with Takahashi-san. I bent over backward to please him and make his life easier whenever I could. I began in earnest for the first time to show real interest in the haikus, fully aware that he seemed slightly disappointed to be the only one writing for the pot.

I took several stabs at composing one at the desk in my room before deciding to make my efforts public, so to speak. It was relatively simple getting the right number of syllables in each line but far more complicated to do so in such a way that the result didn't sound completely banal. In the end I followed Takahashi-san's advice and endeavored to write about a specific thought or emotion, or an event that had left an impression on me, no matter how fleetingly. Not to be too ambitious. To knead a little ball and let it rise in the reader's mind, as he put it.

The sea remained calm
but I could hear waves breaking
somewhere in my head.

I wrote the haiku on a piece of paper which I folded and put in my pocket before I started my lunch shift on Thursday. But dropping it in the pot felt strangely daunting, so I put it off until after lunch. Then I finally took the plunge and deposited the folded slip when nobody was looking, before hurrying off to meet Miko at the café next to her campus.

She could tell I was a little excited. I told her about the haiku.

"It won't change anything," she said.

I asked her what she meant.

"He already likes you; you don't need to ingratiate yourself with him."

"I enjoyed writing it," I said.

She smiled the way people smile at fools. "Good," she said. "But it won't change anything."

When I returned at half past five, the piece of paper was still in the pot. But soon afterward Hitomi discovered it and walked into the kitchen holding it between finger and thumb like a dead fly. "Takahashi-san, look!"

He gave a little start, set aside his knife and pincers, took the piece of paper, opened it, and read. First to himself, then out loud. "Hm," he said, "hm," and went on contemplating the piece of paper in his hand before looking up. "Nice work, Hitomi-san."

"I didn't write it," she said.

"You didn't?"

"No-oh."

"Are you sure?"

"Takahashi-san . . ."

"Not you either, Goto-san?"

Goto-san grinned.

"Who, then?" said Takahashi-san, feigning surprise. "Not you, Kristófer-san?"

I smiled.

"Kristófer-san," said Hitomi, "are you a poet?"

"No," I said.

"Waves breaking in your head," Takahashi-san repeated as if to himself and carried on prepping for dinner. "Amid a calm sea. Yes, it could be. Waves breaking. In your head."

I can't deny feeling quite proud that Takahashi-san should consider my haiku worthy of contemplation. Not that I was foolish enough to start seeing myself as a promising poet or anything, far from it. But I did enjoy playing around with the three lines and seventeen syllables, not least because it made me feel closer to Takahashi-san. It was as if we had created a new language of our own which other people could participate in only as spectators. I thought of him when I composed or, rather, kneaded my haikus, not Hitomi or Steve or Goto-san, or even Miko. Only Takahashi-san. I was showing him what was in my head, maybe as a way of asking his forgiveness or, as Miko had said, to try to impress him in the hope that he might change his mind. And yet I was groping in the dark, for his intentions were a mystery to me, as were the qualities Miko's suitors needed to possess in order to earn his approval.

"What is it?" I asked her one afternoon in my room, unable to contain myself any longer. "What does he want for you? Do you even know?"

That was when she began to weep. She turned away from me, sat on the edge of the bed, and buried her face in her hands. I didn't dare touch her.

"Miko," I managed to gasp.

She said nothing, just dressed in silence and left.

I never asked her again.

I am standing at the well-known crossing at the center of Shibuya, where sidewalks point in every direction, right and left, forward and back, diagonally across the intersection that teems with life beneath the multicolored TV screens and billboards. There is a perpetual hum of voices, laughter and shouts, music emanating from restaurants and shops, the noise of traffic. I come to a halt and accept a flyer from a young man in black who, it seems, works for a nearby electronics store. "Good price," he repeats in English, persistent but polite.

I move along with the flow. I could have taken a shortcut to avoid the crowds, as the restaurants recommended by the young woman at the hotel are away from the center. And yet something attracts me, some desire to enter this human whirlpool, to be in the midst of it. I feel slightly bewildered and have to pause to get my bearings, a bit dazed and not quite sure which crossing I need to take to get where I am headed.

First I am going to try the little *tonkatsu* place, which, according to the map, is only a seven-minute walk east of where I am now. "It's a family-run business," the young woman told me, "there's a high bar overlooking the kitchen, where you can watch the chefs, and three or four tables over by the window. It's discreet, on a narrow side street. Nothing fancy."

When at last I set off again, having found the correct route, I move along quite swiftly. I feel increasingly clearheaded after my evening nap and no longer need to run through the list of the starters in my head to make sure my mind is working properly. I have also stopped fretting over what to say to Sonja and am determined that the answer will present itself in due course.

This place is indeed discreet. I walk past it twice before my phone finally guides me to the entrance beneath a white awning with Japanese characters. I am not so tall that I need to stoop when I enter, but I do so anyway, as the door is low. The young woman at the hotel assured me this wasn't a tourist haunt, and I can see that is true when I get inside and look around. Not that people stare at me, but I certainly stand out among the other guests.

But I am made to feel welcome and shown to a seat by the bar facing the kitchen. My efforts to make myself understood in Japanese probably help, and the woman serving me is clearly impressed, despite my meager vocabulary and clumsy pronunciation.

When I have sat down and begun browsing the menu, she offers me a glass of sake, which I feel I can't refuse, although I rarely drink alcohol these days. I cut down years ago, not because I had a problem but out of solidarity with Inga when she decided she required a thorough overhaul. Those were her words, not mine; she felt she needed to take a good look at several aspects of her life at the time, one of which was her use of alcohol. She also joined a yoga class, changed her diet, and started to think both more deeply and more expansively about things. That was how she described it, and although she occasionally condemned her old lifestyle the way people do when they turn over a new leaf, rather than dwelling on it, she focused more on being kind to herself and contented with her life. She stopped drinking completely and so did I, to keep her company, but I continued to abstain later on, when she became more relaxed about her own use.

There are two chefs who I quickly realize are father and son. At first glance they don't look very much alike, but once I start watching them, it is obvious they are related. Not only do they have the same build, but their gestures and mannerisms are also almost identical. The father is a little more serious-looking but friendly, and he welcomes my decision to put the menu aside and instead to rely on their ingenuity.

"*Osusume*," I say. He gives a quick bow to show he has understood my request.

"Another sake?" asks the woman who greeted me.

I accept because the sake is smooth and aromatic, adequately chilled, and goes down easily. The son passes me a bowl of edamame, followed soon after by a plate of *hiyayakko*, cold tofu with ginger and pickled plum.

"*Itadakimasu*," I say.

The food is excellent, and I can't deny it is pleasant to feel the alcohol in my veins. My mind is agreeably empty; it doesn't wander but lets me be happy with what is in front of me, enjoying the moment. Even so, I pull out my phone to see if Miko has replied at all. She hasn't, but I notice Sonja's messages.

"Did you forget his birthday?"

"March 20."

"Tokyo?"

I decide to respond and tease her a little, good-naturedly, of course, just to see how she reacts.

"Yes," I write.

I am nine hours ahead of Sonja, who is presumably at work. Yet she texts back immediately, and I smile at how predictable her reply is, even the format.

"The birthday or Tokyo?"

She hasn't taken the time, any more than normally, to write a whole sentence, which might read as follows: "Have your forgotten his birthday or are you in Tokyo?" Her impatience is palpable; she clearly finds my reply unamusing and thinks I am being careless or vague at best but more likely apathetic or possibly even slow.

I need to reflect before I reply, and besides, it's rude to be on my phone when there is food being served. I slip it back in my pocket and focus on my meal, which looks delightful.

But since I'm on the subject, this enthusiasm of Sonja's for birthdays, birthday gifts, and birthday parties is most curious. I don't quite understand it, but then, as I've said before, I have never been interested in birthdays, least of all my own, and I actually prefer to ignore them. Not that she shows any interest when it comes to my birthday; her focus is on her and Axel's and Villi's birthdays. And not just the important ones, any old birthday.

Sitting here now, I am able to smile at this obsession of hers because I feel good. But I haven't always felt that way, and perhaps I ought to explain why.

If it were only these demands for gifts she makes in advance, I might not have so much cause for complaint. I am not above buying them birthday presents and might even thank her for reminding me, for saving me the trouble of having to shop, which I find tedious. But not content with demanding specific presents from me, she has somehow reached the conclusion over the years that it's only natural I foot the bill for every birthday celebration.

Maybe I realized this fully only when Axel arrived on the scene. I had met him two or three times, but they had probably been dating for a few months already. She called Torg right before the lunch shift and asked to speak to me. Despite being busy, I went to the phone because it was unusual for her to call me at work unless it was something urgent. For example, when her mother fell down the stairs. But this time I could tell from her voice that there was nothing serious going on.

"Hi, Dad."

"Hello, Sonja."

"Hey, it's Axel's birthday."

"Is that the young man who left his shoes lying in the hallway last night? I nearly broke my neck. They're more like skis."

She decided to laugh. "It's his birthday today."

I waited for what was coming.

"I really want to treat him to a nice dinner. There'll only be six of us."

"What?" I said.

"I want it to be a surprise. He thinks we're just going to the cinema or something."

Sonja was twenty-two at the time. She was no child; she was a student at the university and often spoke about her concerns for the future of mankind.

"Axel's birthday?" I repeated.

"Yes, today. Mozart was born today and Lewis Carroll too. Also Nick Mason, the drummer of Pink Floyd. Axel's a big fan of Pink Floyd, but he didn't know they had the same birthday."

I don't remember what I said. Only that she asked if table twelve was free. She had worked two summers at Torg and was familiar with the table arrangements.

I remember they arrived at eight o'clock. And that they ordered a bottle of white wine and a bottle of red, not the most expensive on the list but not the cheapest either. I remember they each had a starter, a main, and a dessert. I remember Sonja behaving as if she were their host.

I also remember not making a fuss about it and letting her get away with it year after year.

It's probably my own fault that Sonja was so taken aback when I could no longer hold my tongue. It was many years later, on her thirty-first or thirty-second birthday. She went through the usual routine, which I had come to expect, only this time I didn't play along, and when she announced that she was coming with Axel and six guests, I said: "I think this has gone far enough, don't you?"

Naturally she was shocked, and maybe I explained it too carefully, listed too many instances of her demanding, overbearing behavior in the past, even if I didn't use those exact words. She took offense and said maybe she should be thankful to me for finally being honest with her, that it was about time she knew how I really felt about her, or words to that effect.

"So now I know," she said, and hung up.

This evening I can look back at that conversation without the memory of it upsetting me, without reproaching myself for the umpteenth time for not having let it lie. I can smile at the fact that she and not I was cast as the victim. I accept another sake and take up my chopsticks just as the son pushes a fragrant dish of *tonkatsu* along the bar table in front of me.

We had grown so used to concealing our relationship from our colleagues at work that we found it difficult to act differently around
other people. I hadn't told any of my friends about Miko, and she
had told only her friend Elizabeth. We avoided touching even
when it was impossible that anyone we knew would see us, for
example, in cafés or at art galleries, strolling along the river or in
a park, sitting on a bench in a secluded street, or lost in a crowd
in a busy pub. We scarcely dared to hold hands when we went
to the cinema after the lights dimmed and would sit at the back,
where we were least conspicuous. We didn't talk about it; it just
sort of happened that we silently began to behave like criminals
on the run from the law.

She was less averse to sneaking around than I. And yet I didn't
dare bring up the subject for fear she might be tempted to with-
draw, avoid me, end our brief relationship. Instead I reminded
myself that I had never been happier, that I never believed it possible to be this happy, and that should be enough.

All the same I longed to be able to act spontaneously when I was with her, to put my arm around her while we were out walking, tell her how much I loved her, kiss her, even if it was just a peck on the forehead, caress her hand in mine. But Takahashi-san's shadow followed us wherever we went, and it was only behind the locked door of my room in Kensington that we seemed to be free of him.

I often thought that perhaps we needed to get away from the city to be able to escape these constraints. Preferably somewhere nobody knew us, somewhere we had never been before and probably would never go again. Perhaps one day we might move to such a place, I thought, the two of us, spend our lives together there.

It was Miko who told me about the Bath Festival of Blues because Elizabeth was going and had offered Miko her room while she was away if she needed. I had never heard of the festival but did some research and suggested to Miko that she and I go together. The timing was perfect, as Takahashi-san had been forced to close Nippon for a few days to carry out various renovations and repairs he had been putting off, not least on the customer restrooms.

I left ahead of Miko on Friday morning. She and Elizabeth would arrive together in the afternoon. I had booked a room at a B&B in the old part of town and went straight there from the station. It was a beautiful house with five guest rooms, and the couple who ran it couldn't have been nicer. Our room gave onto the garden where a tall tree stood in the middle of the lawn casting an early-morning shadow over the house. I took off my socks and walked out onto the lawn after having settled in. I stood in the warm sunshine with the grass beneath my feet, listening to the birdsong and the echo of my words when I greeted the owners: "My girlfriend is arriving by train later today."

I marveled at the freedom those words entailed. They came

naturally to me, as if I uttered them all the time and had nothing to hide.

And the couple both smiled because the anticipation in my voice was palpable, my joy as luminous as the sunlight in the garden.

Miko and Elizabeth arrived shortly before five. I met them off the train, and Miko and I embraced on the platform as if it were perfectly normal. Outside on the street we said goodbye to Elizabeth, who was meeting friends of hers who lived in Bath.

In the evening we went out to dinner. It was warm; we sat outside on the sidewalk. Afterward we took a stroll around the city holding hands, and she played the guide, having done some research before she came. I enjoyed seeing the churches and bridges, the old houses and towers, the Roman baths, the gardens and squares, but everything paled in comparison to just being with her.

That night she fell asleep in my arms. I lay awake and listened to her breathing. In the morning I contemplated the shadow of the tree across the window before being forced to give her a nudge.

We ate brunch in the garden. The sun was still shining. I was tempted to delay when the time came for us to leave for the festival, which started at noon and continued until the evening. The festival was held at the Recreational Ground, a large open space in the center of town, not far from the River Avon. We left in good time, maybe out of a slight sense of duty but also with a flutter of excitement at the prospect of being free among all those people.

A host of legendary bands played at the festival—I remember, for example, Fleetwood Mac, John Mayall & the Bluesbreakers, Chicken Shack, and Led Zeppelin. I should mention that I had never heard of the group Chicken Shack and didn't hear much of them afterward, but the name stuck in my mind.

We were blessed with good weather, although a few clouds gathered over the city in the afternoon with a brief downpour. Miko's hair got soaked and took on a pale blue luster as it dried.

Toward evening I walked into town to buy bread, cheese, cold cuts, and fruit for us to eat. We had spread a rug on the grass near a stand of trees, not too close to the stage, and Miko waited there for me while I went to the shops. We were surrounded by happy people, and somebody called us John and Yoko. It was so innocent and good-natured that we just laughed. I remember when I got back, she stood up and flung her arms around me, looked inside the bag, and said, "Oh, how wonderful!" as if I had done this sort of thing often and would do it again. Stroll to the shops to buy us something to eat.

That evening we made love. It was different from before. No wall came crashing down between us or anything; more like the thinnest of screens was torn asunder. We became one. Nothing separated us. I disappeared into her and she into me.

Afterward she told me about her mother. I hadn't asked; it wouldn't have occurred to me to bring up anything that might upset her. We were lying quietly in the dark, she was running her fingers through my hair. And then she said, as though picking up a conversation we had been having, softly but without hesitation: "They lived in Kure. But Mom was visiting her parents in Hiroshima that day. Hiroshima is about an hour from Kure. She was six months pregnant. She'd just stopped having morning sickness. She was twenty-three, Dad was ten years older. He was a teacher. You didn't know that, did you?"

"No," I said.

"He taught in primary school. But it was the summer holidays. Dad and a few others were repairing the school roof when the bomb fell. Nobody knew what had happened; some thought there had been a gas explosion. Later that day Dad joined a crowd of people going to Hiroshima. On the way, they came across a team of horses standing by the side of the road. They looked normal, except their bellies were so swollen they dragged along the ground.

"I don't know how he managed to find Grandma and Grandpa's house. He says he has no memory of it. Only of the scorched earth, the incandescent sky, and the black rain. And the river filled with corpses.

"Mom was badly burned. He took her to the hills around the city, where he tended to her. There were no medics. They had died, just like the rest. Those who had survived were searching for their relatives. Mom was clasping Grandma's arm when he found her.

"She gave birth to me a month prematurely. She died a year later."

Miko fell silent. I knew she wouldn't continue; she had said everything she wanted to say. Perhaps everything she knew. But then she added, lowering her voice even more: "Yet I'm still a *hibakusha*."

A moment later she was asleep. But I lay awake, filled with the same anger I had felt at the library, anger and impotence. I held her as close as I could without waking her.

When she opened her eyes in the morning, she smiled and kissed me. She got out of bed and opened the door to the garden, stretched, embraced the day, and said something about the sunshine. It was as if her telling of the story a few hours earlier had never happened.

The train is hurtling south. It is three o'clock. I sit by the window watching buildings and mountains rush by, bridges and rivers, cranes and warehouses. The city disappears, giving way to golden fields, forests in the distance. Then another city, suburbs, still more cranes. I am on the Shinkansen bullet train, which moves at such speed that the journey takes only four hours—or 233 minutes, as it says in the brochure I picked up at the hotel before checking out. It also gives the distance: 894.2 kilometers. Japanese rail workers are punctual, and as the train left bang on time, I expect to arrive at my destination not a minute too late or too soon. That will be at four minutes past six.

I still haven't heard from Miko and I still manage to convince myself I needn't worry. My head feels a bit heavy after last night, but I have only myself to blame, as I am not used to drinking and should have gone easy on the sake. However, it's been a while since I slipped the traces, so to speak, and I don't regret my moment of recklessness. Not that I went overboard, far from it, though I did let go a little, and even rediscovered my singing voice, which, if I say so myself, wasn't bad once upon a time. Back then I belonged to the choir, where I met Inga, but that's another story.

I won't blame Kutaragi-san from Osaka for what happened, although if he hadn't shown up, I certainly would have returned to the hotel a lot earlier. I was halfway through my meal when he appeared and sat down next to me, at arm's length, as required, and took off his face mask. He was about the same age, smartly dressed in a gray suit and a white shirt unbuttoned at the neck. I instantly saw he was talkative and seemed on friendly terms with the staff. It turned out he was a regular, making frequent trips to the city to visit his son and his son's family. He was retired and a widower. He soon turned toward me and introduced himself in good English, a language I suspect he enjoyed speaking and tried to maintain.

We hadn't been chatting for long when I found out that he had worked in London in the late sixties and early seventies, for Mitsubishi Corporation. Indeed, he had been with the company his entire working life, as is the custom here. Starting as a salary-man, he had worked his way up gradually until he was given a post abroad, first as manager in a small division and subsequently as general manager at a larger one, then director, and finally vice president. His first job when he arrived in London was to oversee the sale of oil to European shipping companies whose vessels needed to refuel at Japanese ports. After that he moved to steel imports. He described his job in great detail, how many tons Mitsubishi sold to British manufacturers of transformers, his elation after two years in the job when imports reached as high as six or seven thousand tons, I don't recall which. "Nineteen seventy-one," he said, "under my management. Forty percent market share."

The anecdote wasn't as tedious as it might have been, and he didn't draw it out. He undoubtedly lived a little in the past and seemed nostalgic about his time in London, Paris, and Amsterdam before the company sent him to America, where he worked for a decade. Naturally we spoke mostly about his years in London, because he became very excited when I told him I myself had lived there during that time.

For some reason I decided to tell him only about having been a student there and mentioned neither my job at Nippon nor at the restaurant where I worked subsequently. Admittedly I played down my studies and said nothing about quitting the university he correctly described as "prestigious and highly respected." But I answered him truthfully when he asked which subject I had studied, and we went on to talk a bit about economics, because that was what his son had studied at university.

"He's doing very well for himself," he said. "Assistant managing director of internal communications at Matsushita. He enjoys their growing confidence in him."

I took the opportunity to ask him more about his son as a way of drawing the conversation away from myself and my days in London.

Kutaragi-san was a gourmand and particularly fond of sake. He was indeed something of a sake connoisseur and wished to correct what he called a general misconception, although I had said nothing that could be considered controversial. Nevertheless, he was keen to enlighten me, and the best way to do this, in his opinion, was for us to sample different sakes and then discuss the differences between them. I can't recall just this minute everything he said, although I could definitely see what he meant when he used the expression "night and day" and others like it. Some were a little acidic, others sweet, still others so smooth that I emptied my glass without realizing. He repeatedly asked the father and son for their opinion, and they agreed heartily with his judgments, indicating that they didn't think he was exaggerating

at all, and even raised a glass with us once we were the only customers left at the bar table.

It's no wonder I got a little tipsy or that my tongue loosened as the night wore on. Thus, I responded openly when he
asked why I had come to Japan—or more precisely, what drew
me to Hiroshima, for I had already told him that was where I was
headed.

"I'm going to visit a woman friend of mine," I said.

"Is she Japanese?"

"Yes," I said, adding: "I met her when I lived in London."

"In London?"

"Yes," I said.

"Was she also a student at LSE?"

"No," I said, "she worked in a restaurant."

He looked at me inquiringly.

"Yes," I said, "at Nippon."

"Nippon? Really?"

It was probably thanks to the sake that my pulse didn't quicken
and I was able to casually ask him if he had ever eaten there.

"It had already closed by the time I came to London, just
before Christmas in sixty-nine," he said. "But people still talked
about it. I remember Nobukazu-san said he missed it."

And that was all. He reiterated what a small world it was,
the way people often do when some coincidence strikes them as
meaningful, and I didn't contradict him.

We were both quite drunk when we stood up to pay. Kutaragi-
san insisted on paying for the sake we had sampled together and
wouldn't take no for an answer despite my protestations. As a
result, I felt indebted to him when we left and couldn't refuse
when he asked if I would like to have a nightcap with him at one
of his favorite bars, an old-style tavern. It was a tiny little place
with only a few tables, the entrance down a narrow, secluded alleyway. Kutaragi-san was given a warm reception by the owner,

a middle-aged man who offered us a shot of Japanese whiskey that smelled of honey and cedarwood. We sipped slowly, and Kutaragi-san went on talking about his son as if he felt he hadn't exhausted the subject back at the restaurant. It turned out he was a little worried about him and shared his concerns with me. He even asked my advice, which, alas, I was unable to offer, as I don't have his experience of international business affairs.

Kutaragi-san was afraid that his son wasn't ambitious enough; he thought he should have moved further up the company ladder and should be making more of an effort to get promoted out of his department. He said he had tried to explain to his son that if times got tough, he risked getting laid off, and urged him to seek a transfer, preferably to one of the more flourishing divisions. His son listened politely but ignored his father's advice, smiling as if to say his old man was stuck in the past and things were different now.

"He's nearly forty and yet he talks like he's a child," said Kutaragi-san. "About how important it is to keep staff informed, to encourage and be honest with them." He sighed. "When things get tough, they will inform him, all right, that his services are no longer required; that's all the honesty he can expect."

Clearly Kutaragi-san was speaking from experience, although I couldn't work out which side he was speaking from. Nor did I ask, and then he turned the conversation to Sonja.

"What about your daughter?" he said. "Is she ambitious?"

"You could say that," I said, and smiled.

"Good," he replied.

"Maybe," I said.

"Oh?"

I told him about the text messages, the birthday parties, her demands. I think I managed to strike a lighthearted note, and yet he looked a little pensive.

"How will you reply?"

"Sorry?"

"To her question about whether you're in Tokyo or have forgotten her son's birthday. You haven't yet, have you?"

"Later," I said, and when Kutaragi-san looked surprised, I added: "I have no problem telling her I'm in Tokyo, but I'm less keen to admit that I completely forgot her son's birthday."

Kutaragi-san patted me on the back. "I know how you feel," he said. "I don't find it funny when Masahiko implies I am constantly fighting ghosts from the past that nobody else cares about. I don't find it funny at all."

We quietly sipped our whiskey, allowing our minds to accommodate these disclosures. And then Kutaragi-san sat up, clapped me on the back once more, and said cheerily: "It's always good to sing when you need cheering up."

He rose to his feet and had a word with the owner, who gave a little bow before opening a door at the back of the bar and switching on the lights in a small room. In it stood four chairs and a table by the wall with an old television set on it. The owner left us, pulling the door closed behind him. Kutaragi-san turned on the television.

"Karaoke," he said. "Not the latest equipment, but we have the place to ourselves. Do you remember 'Sukiyaki'?"

It was years since I'd heard that song last, but it came back to me in a flash. It had been a hit in the early sixties, the first Japanese song to top the charts in the West.

Kutaragi-san removed his jacket and cast it aside, picked up the microphone, and sat down on a chair in front of the screen. From the very first line, he managed to evoke a sense of longing and regret. I followed the lyrics, which appeared on the screen in Japanese and in English: *I look up as I walk so the tears won't fall, remembering those spring days, but I am all alone tonight.*

Evidently this wasn't the first time Kutaragi-san had sung "Sukiyaki." He didn't look at the screen but got up and sang with his eyes shut, moving his head from side to side; it was like watching a tree sway in the breeze.

I look up as I walk counting the stars with tearful eyes . . . Happiness lies beyond the clouds . . .

He sat still as the music trailed off and didn't stir until we had listened to the silence for a while, to the song echoing in our head. Then he cleared his throat twice.

"'Sukiyaki.' Kyu Sakamoto," he said, and handed me the microphone. "What would you like to sing?"

I hadn't intended to sing, but I took the microphone from him and studied the song list on the screen.

"'Yesterday,'" I said tentatively, then with more resolve. "Yes, 'Yesterday.'"

I hadn't sung publicly in a long time, and at first I didn't recognize the voice filling the small room. I had the sensation that I was listening to someone else sing about yesterday, someone older and wearier than I was.

I wasn't halfway through the song when I felt my eyes fill with tears. I tried to wipe them away, but it was no use, so I let them flow freely. It didn't affect my voice and I finished the song passably well, to judge from Kutaragi-san's response, for he stood up and bowed before clearing his throat again and declaring in the tone of a radio announcer: "'Yesterday.' The Beatles."

We sang no more songs and soon afterward found ourselves out on the street, where we embraced before parting, with no thought for viruses and epidemics, simply grateful to have found a friend when in need, our eyes moist with tears, each dragging the ghosts from our past in our wake.

Miko and I took the train back late on Sunday afternoon. It was full of young people like us who had attended the festival, some still carrying the music in their head, especially the couple behind us, who played guitar and sang nearly the entire journey. We had spent the day in town, strolling through streets and gardens, eating lunch on a bench by the river, lying in the sun on a grassy patch. She hadn't said anything more about her mother, and I knew not to ask. But I had memorized the word *hibakusha* and finally wrote it down discreetly so as not to forget.

Before the train even ground to a halt in Paddington Station, I noticed a change in her. She pulled her hand free of mine, reached into the linen pouch she used as a bag, and pretended to rummage for something before replacing her hand in her lap until we stood up. Not daring to put my arm around her or behave the way I had all weekend in Bath, I held back. We barely kissed when we said goodbye.

They finished the renovations at Nippon on Tuesday. I helped out on Monday, painted the restrooms and assisted the carpenter and the plumber, cleaned up after them. But I also went to the library to look up the word *hibakusha* and read every article I could find on the subject. They were fewer than I had expected.

I discovered it was the name given to survivors of the bombings of Hiroshima and Nagasaki. In one of the articles was an interview with a woman and a man, both of whom had suffered severe burns as well as radiation poisoning during the attack on Hiroshima but somehow survived. There were photographs of the woman's back, covered with scars, and the man's disfigured legs. I found it hard to look at them and to read the accompanying descriptions, although they weren't in any way sensationalist.

You couldn't see the faces of the people in any of the photographs, and no names appeared. No explanation was given. I discovered the reason for this later.

I didn't see Miko until Thursday afternoon. We had arranged to meet at my place, and I rushed back home after lunch. I got there before her and waited in our usual place on the corner. She arrived soon after and we hurried up to my room.

We drew the curtains, took off our clothes, and crawled into bed. My head was filled with our nights in Bath, and I longed to recapture them when I really should have let them reside peacefully in my memory. I knew this, yet I couldn't help myself and even repeated some of what I had said to her as we lay entwined, the garden door thrown open and the light from the half-moon streaming in. But Miko said nothing, wouldn't play along, just placed her finger on my lips and sat astride me.

It was as if she had a need to take charge. I didn't mind and submitted willingly. But she took a long time to climax, and I had difficulty controlling myself and had to ask her to stop. I couldn't help suspecting she was doing this on purpose, for she taunted me as she sat still on top of me, taunted me and then slowly started moving again. "Can't you handle it?"

I don't mean she was trying to belittle me. She was never like that; in fact, her teasing made me even more excited, to the point where I had to ask her to pause again. Then she smiled, leaned forward and kissed me, told me to open my eyes, and gazed into them silently, a faint smile lingering on her lips.

We both had to go back to work—I to the restaurant, she to the lab—and yet she dressed in more of a hurry than necessary and then waited impatiently by the door for me to get ready. I had decided to talk to her about what I had read in the library, so when she grasped the door handle, I asked if she could wait a minute.

"What is it?" she said.

What did you mean when you said "Yet"? I had planned to ask.

Yet what? I imagined her replying.

When you said: Yet I'm still a hibakusha . . .

I had gone over it enough times in my head and was convinced this was the right approach. And yet looking at her there by the door as she clasped the handle, seemingly anxious to leave, I lost my courage.

"Nothing," I said, grabbing my keys and following her down the stairs and out onto the street.

Afterward I was certain she had read my mind, had guessed I would want to discuss what she had told me about her mother, and behaved accordingly from the moment we met on the corner outside the hairdresser's. It explained her desire to take control while we were in my room and why she hadn't opened even the smallest window into her head or heart. Why she was in such a hurry to leave.

I often felt remorse when I went back to Nippon after being with Miko at my house, but never more so than now. I could scarcely look Takahashi-san in the eye and kept my head down. In contrast, he was in good spirits, delighted with the renovations and equally pleased about being able to reopen. This made it even harder for me to be around him.

"What's wrong with you?" Hitomi whispered to me.

I gave a start.

"Haven't you noticed there's a piece of paper in the pot?"

I hadn't. No more than I had anything else around me. But I went to the bar, pulled it out, and read:

A stream in a field?
No, only water splashing
from a brand-new tap.

Takahashi-san had evidently been waiting for me to look in the pot and now watched me read out of the corner of his eye. I mustered a smile and made some comment about the poem just to please him, but with an effort. He seemed oblivious and made a joke about Hitomi having composed the haiku and that we had to watch out.

"Fierce competition," he said. "How are you going to respond, Kristófer-san? It's your turn."

It was then that the haiku I couldn't show them came to life effortlessly in my head. I didn't have to do anything; it emerged by itself and hasn't changed since.

The stars do flicker
yet in my heaven your eyes
shine brightest of all.

I didn't write it down, I never have. But I remember it most mornings along with my ID card number, my bank account number, the menu, and the names of the Icelandic presidents.

I find a piece of paper in my jacket pocket from last night. I puzzle over it for a few seconds, but then it all comes back to me. It was Kutaragi-san who was given it by the son at the restaurant, and then jotted down on it something about sake that I had difficulty memorizing. *Futsu-shu*, *tokutei meisho-shu*, each word underlined twice. I remember him explaining how all sake is classified as either *futsu-shu* or *tokutei meisho-shu*, but I have no idea which he said was supposedly the superior one. He neglected to write that down, presumably thinking I wouldn't forget.

One hour left to go. I didn't take up the hotel's offer of a complimentary meal, as I wasn't hungry and instead, before the train left, bought a bento box at Tokyo Station and have been picking at it throughout the journey. It is simple but good food: rice balls, tempura prawns, pickled vegetables, noodles. I have dozed off a few times and came to just now, for example, thinking I still haven't replied to Sonja.

I didn't intend to put it off last night, but by the time I got back to the hotel, I was too tired. It was after one in the morning, as I got a bit lost on the way and had to ask directions when I couldn't follow them on my phone. Although it was late, I wanted to thank the young woman at reception for recommending such a good restaurant, so after having my temperature taken at the entrance, I went straight over to the front desk. She had gone home, but the young man who had taken over from her promised to pass on the message.

Rice paddies, sloping hills in the distance, a small lake, a village at the foot of a mountain. I switch on my phone and reply to Sonja, saying that I am on my way to Hiroshima and that I forgot Villi's birthday. No beating about the bush, no apology for my oversight or any other comment, although I do send my regards to both Villi and Axel.

"I am watching rice paddies whoosh by," I write. "The sky is partially clouded and the forecast tonight is for torrential rain. In Tokyo I saw the cherry blossom."

Inga died seven years ago today. It occurs to me to say something in my message to Sonja, to preempt her so she won't be able to accuse me of not remembering. But I decide against it, because worrying about it seems a bit exaggerated, and it's ungenerous of me to think she would go that far.

Inga's death came after a long illness. I always feel sad when I think about it and prefer to look back to the time when we got to know each other, because she was so cheerful and fun to be with, the life and soul of the party, especially in our choir.

She had been in the choir for a few years when I joined. I let myself be persuaded by my friend Daniel; it was his way of introducing me to people, as he put it. Daniel was a fine lyric baritone with a high tessitura. He came to work for me at Torg soon after we opened, and all he knew of my vocal prowess was from hearing me sing along to my favorite tunes on the radio.

I was in my early forties and finally thinking about settling down, as it's called. I was welcomed by the other choir members, men and women, and quickly discovered that I enjoyed the company.

I noticed Inga the very first day. She was very attractive but didn't flaunt it. Her charm lay in her sociability and a certain lack of inhibition which came out in her singing. I learned that she was divorced and had a young daughter, ran a boutique on Laugarvegur with another woman and was herself an accomplished dressmaker, lived on Bragagata, and was five years younger than I.

I started to look forward to seeing her at choir practice. It was strange, experiencing those emotions again, and at first I didn't really know what was happening. I began sprucing myself up before choir practice; I put on aftershave, a clean shirt, polished my shoes. She and I would go for coffee afterward. I invited her out to dinner. We went for a stroll around Lake Tjörnin; I spent the night at her place. Three months later she left Bragagata and moved in with me.

It wasn't long before I started wondering if I hadn't made a terrible mistake. I remember it was a Saturday morning in May when it first happened. We were in the kitchen, and she was talking about her ex-husband, Orri. Sonja was meant to be spending the weekend with him but, as was often the case, something had cropped up. I listened, nodded occasionally—too bad we wouldn't make it to the theater—and poured her a cup of coffee. The radio was on, a music program with people talking in between songs. I wasn't paying much attention, and their voices mingled with Inga's carping and the window rattling in the breeze. Then suddenly I gave a start; a new song had come on that forced out all other sounds, so I didn't hear a word of what Inga was saying, much less the wind outside—"Julia" by the Beatles, Lennon's song. I stood mesmerized, holding the cup of coffee and only vaguely aware of Inga raising her voice, evidently not for the first time: "Kristófer, Kristófer, is something the matter?" I finally recovered my senses and looked at her as if seeing her for the first time, as if she had stepped in off the street and installed herself in my flat like an intruder.

Then I realized. Then I realized I had made a terrible mistake.

It was entirely my fault, not hers. She deserved better, a man who loved her unconditionally and enjoyed her company, who never had any doubts and looked forward in his sleep to waking beside her every morning, who never dreamed of another woman. She'd had plenty of suitors after she and Orri divorced, including at least two from the choir. And yet she chose me, that was her misfortune.

I tried. I did my best, but it wasn't enough. She knew something was wrong, she sensed what was missing, I couldn't hide that. We had been living together only a few months when, one morning as we were leaving the house, she asked me if I regretted "this." I don't remember the context, maybe there wasn't one, and she gave a little laugh as if to make light of her question. I knew exactly what she was referring to, obviously, and felt she didn't deserve me not to acknowledge that. "Of course not, how could you think such a thing?" I heard myself say, the words sounding hollow and false.

I should have replied honestly but instead, a week later, in a fit of remorse, I asked her to marry me.

We were married in the autumn. She arranged everything. A hundred guests attended our wedding, and Inga looked so beautiful that I nearly wept because I knew what I was doing to her. "Do you, Kristófer Hannesson, insist upon wrecking Inga Karlsdóttir's life by taking her as your wife?"

That was what the priest's words sounded like to me in Reykjavík Cathedral. He looked me straight in the eye and so did Inga, and as soon as he had finished reading the vows, I said in a very loud voice: "I do," because I didn't want anyone to see how I was feeling. There was laughter in the church, as people found my enthusiasm touching and sweet, and afterward Daniel said: "You were sure in a hurry, you didn't want to let her get away, did you?"

Seven years since she died and not a day goes by when I don't beg her forgiveness.

"I am watching rice paddies whoosh by. In Tokyo I saw the cherry blossom . . ."

I send Sonja the text, put my phone back in my bag, and close my eyes. We have about half an hour to go. Maybe I will manage to forget myself for a while.

I hadn't seen Jói Steinsson in several weeks. I assumed he must have gotten a summer job in Iceland, because lectures finished in May, and after that the dorms emptied. The summer before, he had worked at the National Statistical Institute of Iceland, and when school started in September, he'd regaled us with stories about his colleagues. Needless to say, he made fun of them, referred to their incompetence, mimicked them calculating the inflation rate, which they were always surprised to discover was still rocketing. "Oh dear," he would say, scratching his head and grimacing, "forty-two point three percent. We have to do something . . ." And then add: "You were better off going to sea, Kristófer," even though he knew perfectly well that I had gotten a job on a fishing boat only because I needed the money and would have far rather worked at the Institute or somewhere I could apply my knowledge and gain some experience.

I didn't miss university and hadn't thought about Jói Steinsson at all. Shortly after I quit, a mutual acquaintance had confided to me over a beer that Jói had been making fun of me, but I shrugged it off. If I remember correctly, he was supposed to have said the only thing we achieved with our student rebellion was that I ended up washing dishes; long live socialism, and so on.

So I was taken aback when, one Friday evening in July, Miko came into the kitchen and told me some customers had come in who said they knew me. "Icelanders," she said, "they asked about you." It was around seven o'clock and the kitchen was busy. I asked her to tell them that I would pop out and see them when I had a minute. In the meantime, I was able to peer into the dining room, where I saw Jói and Marteinn Hauksson. I had been at grammar school with Marteinn, and to the best of my knowledge, he was studying at the University of Iceland, so I assumed he must be visiting. I was also aware that he and Jói had grown up together in the Laugarnes neighborhood of Reykjavík and were old friends.

I won't deny I was nervous about meeting them. Particularly Marteinn, who had always looked up to me and frequently sought my help when he was having difficulty with his studies, especially science. Nor did I have much interest in talking to Jói, as I knew his passion for Japanese cuisine hadn't brought him here; it was just so he could say he had seen me washing dishes and make fun of me and my socialism. "If we all end up washing dishes and mopping floors, we'll all be equal," I could hear him say. "Kristófer has clearly figured it out."

I took my time. Fifteen minutes went by, then half an hour. Miko could see I wasn't in any hurry and raised an eyebrow but said nothing. I shrugged and tried to appear that I wasn't anxious at all; just couldn't be bothered, had other things on my mind. But the time came when I could no longer put it off, so I discarded the tea towel, took off my apron, and hung it on a peg. But I paused by the kitchen door at the last moment and turned around, put my apron back on, grabbed the tea towel, and tucked it into the apron strings.

Jói saw me approach; Marteinn had his back to me. But he could see from looking at Jói that I was coming, because he suddenly looked over his shoulder and grinned rather sheepishly.

We said hello. I did my best to appear at ease and was determined to start the conversation. I asked Marteinn what he was doing in London. He said he was on holiday and would be going to Paris next. I asked if he was still studying history. He told me he had changed majors after his first year and was now studying for a law degree.

"How about you?" I said to Jói. "I thought you'd be home in Iceland."

Jói said he had gotten a summer job in the Economics Department and a research grant.

"Which professor are you working for?" I asked.

He said the professor's name. It was the Swede who had annoyed him so much, and with whom he had clashed several times during lectures, somewhat to the awe of the other students.

"Not Engström!"

"Yes," he said.

"Congratulations," I said.

He tried to look nonchalant and I made no further comment. Even so, Marteinn sensed something and looked at each of us in turn, but neither of us said anything.

"And you're working here," Marteinn said.

"Yes," I said.

"How do you like it?"

"It's great."

"You're taking a break from university . . ."

"A break? No, I've quit."

Marteinn feigned surprise but glanced at Jói, who presumably had filled him in. "Really?"

"Yes," I said.

"Why?"

"I realized I could never compete with Jói," I said.

They both laughed rather awkwardly.

"There aren't positions for everyone at the Institute," I added gratuitously.

Jói winced. "That was just last summer," he said.

Miko came over to clear away their empty plates. She could have left it a bit longer, but I think she was slightly curious. They ordered dessert. She went away again.

"Jói tells me you've started to cook here now."

"Yes," explained Jói, "Bill told me he's been here for break-fast."

"No, I just wash dishes," I said.

"Really? But Bill told me . . ."

"He must have misunderstood," I said.

Miko brought over their desserts. I took the opportunity to say my goodbyes. "Back to washing dishes," I said. "Yours. Enjoy your dessert."

Back in the kitchen, I felt drained. I leaned over the sink, opened the cold tap, and splashed water on my face. Straightening up again, I noticed Miko standing behind me. Takahashi-san and Steve were looking for something in the pantry, and I could hear the murmur of their voices. She looked around, then walked up to me, took my hand, and gave it a little squeeze.

I seldom saw Jói around town after that. And I soon forgot his and Marteinn's visit to Nippon, as it was scarcely memorable.

And so I was all the more astonished that Jói should bring it up when we bumped into each other last year on Tryggvagata. I knew by then that he was ill.

"I always admired you for following your dreams," he said.

I couldn't believe my ears.

"Marteinn and I were remembering the other day when we visited you at that Japanese restaurant," he said. "We were talking about the way you rejected everything that prevented you from devoting yourself to what you felt passionate about. That took some guts."

He had grown emaciated and his voice was rather frail. I probably should have rejoiced at his words, but they made me feel bad. I never imagined that one day I would pity Jói Steinsson, or that he would ever have any doubts, however slight, least of all about himself.

"You and Marteinn have done well for yourselves," I said, to change the subject.

"Yes," Jói said. "Neither of us really has anything to complain about."

I seconded that, both there with him on Tryggvagata and at his funeral the other day, when the priest talked about volume indexes, price indexes, income approaches, national accounts, determination, the family, the terraced house in Fossvogur. We had nothing to complain about, I said to myself then. None of us.

Yet at the same time a feeling of doubt had stolen up on me, and hard as I tried, I couldn't push it aside. Not while the priest was speaking or the choir was singing, not afterward when I walked home and looked at the light on Lake Tjörnin, not that night when I was lying in bed. I couldn't find the words to articulate that doubt, which was perhaps the worst part, because it's impossible to deal with thoughts that haven't been put into words, impossible to overcome or dismiss them. I wasn't sure if it was related to Jói or to me or perhaps to both of us, our fates or our lives, which suddenly seemed so terribly brief when I remembered the piggyback he gave me to Trafalgar Square. But then thankfully it melted away, and when I awoke the next day, I reminded myself that I always feel a little peculiar after attending the funerals of my peers.

Gunnar the headwaiter made it out of quarantine and was able to help me find the flat in which I am now installed. He is well acquainted with the website, as he and his husband, Svanur, have used it extensively when traveling both at home and abroad, and they know how to pick and choose. He asked me where in the city I wanted to stay and, before I knew it, had pulled up a map of the area and found several available apartments, some just a few minutes' walk from the Peace Memorial Park, others in the vicinity of the castle. I asked if he could narrow the search, as I wanted to be close to the river but also within walking distance of Miko's house, preferably somewhere quiet. I was afraid I might be asking too much, but Gunnar showed me three places he thought met those requirements, several photographs of each as well as detailed descriptions. They all looked equally attractive, and I had difficulty deciding, so I asked Gunnar to choose for me. He took his mission seriously, reexamined them all, and listed the pros and cons for me before making up his mind. He paid with my credit card and sent the owner a picture of my passport taken on my phone, which presumably is what the rules require.

When I compare the pictures on the website with the actual flat, I see that the owner has given an honest description of every part of it. The flat is bright and clean, the furniture simple but attractive, the washing machine, as indicated, next to the brand-new bathroom. There is a balcony off the living room with a view over the river. Internet. Towels in the cupboard.

On the website there were pictures of blue pillows on the sofa in the living room, an electric kettle in the kitchen and crockery on the dining room table, a bag of coffee with "Café de Coffee" on it, a microwave, a potted plant on the coffee table in the living room—details the owner clearly wanted prospective tenants to see. Every object is in its place, and contemplating them now, I have a sudden sensation of déjà vu that I know every inch of the place, almost as if I've come home. For this is how I feel, not that I am in a foreign country where I don't speak the language or understand the customs but, rather, that I have arrived at home.

It doesn't take long for me to unpack my suitcase, put my clean clothes in the wardrobe, and throw the dirty ones in the washing machine, which I won't actually be running until later. I go about things in a leisurely manner, fill the kettle, switch it on, open the doors to the balcony. A warm breeze wafts in, carrying with it the voices of people on the street and the quiet hum of cars, the rattle of a cart dragged by two men on the sidewalk across the street. I remove the tea towel and the plastic wrapping from my teacup, relieved to see that it hasn't been damaged during the journey, not that I thought it would be, with all the precautions I took. It looks at home next to the kettle, and I can easily imagine it in one of the photographs on the website.

It is less than ten minutes' walk from here to her house. Down along the river, onto a one-way street for a short stretch, then left onto a small square. There stands the building, five floors, not dissimilar to the one I am staying in, to judge from the photograph Gunnar showed me on the computer. I didn't ask him to, but he was so quick with the keyboard that he had already found it before I had time to tell him not to trouble himself.

"This is where your friends live," he said.

I put on my glasses and contemplated the house. It was unremarkable, white painted walls, medium-size windows, small balconies. The photograph was taken at midday; the sun was high in the sky.

"Do you know which floor?" he asked.

"Second," I said.

He enlarged the image and pointed at the screen: "It's one of those two flats; there seem to be two on each floor."

Less than ten minutes. And yet I hesitate, walk out onto the balcony, and look down at the river as if I need to take precautions and preview the route before setting out. I pour hot water into the cup and then dip a tea bag into it, pick up my phone. She still hasn't replied, so I read through her messages again as if to make sure I haven't missed something.

"I live in an apartment building. It's not big. A friend brings me food, she leaves it outside my door. We speak through the window too."

She doesn't go on Facebook much and hasn't thought to post any images or comments about herself. I get the impression she is new to social media, but obviously I can't know that for sure. Some years ago it occurred to me to search for her, but unsurprisingly I didn't find her. Her name is Miko Nakamura now. Not Takahashi but Nakamura.

It crossed my mind to ask her to send me a photograph of herself, but I haven't pursued it. I haven't posted many photographs on my page, a few of the dining room and kitchen at Torg, one of a sunset in Skagafjörður, but that was when I first signed up for Facebook and felt obliged to do the same as everybody else. I am also rather feeble at posting comments about what I am doing, my opinions about this or that, and have never bothered to fill in the profile about my hobbies and interests. I understand well why she might choose to be discreet about herself on social media, and I imagine she probably uses Facebook the way I do, mainly to send messages.

"I always meant to find you again but then time passed and it became too late . . ."

This doesn't sound like she wrote it. Somehow it isn't like her. Maybe the sentence is too long. Too formal. But then I remind myself that I last saw her half a century ago. Over half a century ago, I tell myself again, as if I have just discovered something that wasn't self-evident. I get that sinking feeling and start to tremble slightly, since the obvious thought dawns on me as I stand here holding my teacup that, while the cup may not have changed, Miko is almost certainly a completely different person from who she was when I imagined us spending the rest of our lives together.

I sit. I set down the cup. I glance at the clock as if it might tell me something about the decades that have passed, give me some clue as to where that time went, reveal certain mysteries. But it simply goes on ticking on the wall, measuring seconds and minutes, reminding me that it's evening.

I had contemplated buying her flowers once I finished unpacking. I kept mulling it over on the train, whether it was the right thing to do, and finally decided I couldn't go to her empty-handed. I had the box of chocolates, but somehow they didn't seem suitable for a first visit. I told myself the bouquet mustn't be too big and that I would rather buy a smaller one and be more selective about the flowers. I had even located a nearby florist that stays open until nine, which felt like a big achievement. But now I am too drowsy and weak to stand on my feet, too tired to reassure myself that this trip is anything other than a terrible mistake, the fantasy of an aging man who doesn't always know if he is awake or asleep, who every day needs to make sure his brain hasn't ceased functioning properly. I watch the darkness descend and haven't the energy even to get up and turn on the lights, not until I hear the door phone ring out in the hallway, then I almost jump to my feet.

I am trying to place the events of the summer of '69 in the right sequence, for it has proved challenging to put those weeks into some sort of order in my head. I find it more difficult than remembering my ID card number and names of presidents, starter menus, old poems about stars and eyes. Later, when I tried to make sense of everything, I sometimes had the impression that happenstance or destiny alone had been in control of events, for if Miko's behavior seemed unpredictable at the time, in hindsight it was incomprehensible. Indeed, I had no inkling of what was about to happen and subsequently could find nothing that pointed to it, no matter how hard I racked my brain, almost to the point of obsession. In retrospect, there was no eureka moment, no single thing that should have caused me to stop in my tracks and see what was about to happen; instead it was like a tide coming in so slowly and erratically that you might have thought it was actually going out.

I am referring to the weeks in July and August. For some

reason I always associate the beginning with when Grandma fell ill and was taken to the hospital. Although I could just as well relate it to the moon landing, to the night when we stayed up to watch the BBC broadcast and I couldn't understand why she was so unimpressed.

However, I shall begin with Grandma Klara. She was my father's mother, raised in the east of Iceland, a widow since my grandpa died a few years earlier. She continued to live in their house on Hávallagata, was relatively independent, and had never been ill in her life. Until now, and my mother felt she should write and tell me this, although she insisted Grandma was putting on a brave face and the doctors were hopeful. "It's her heart," Mom wrote, "the arteries." I had always been close to Grandma Klara and would often take the bus to her house when I was a child and later, as a teenager. She would feed me pancakes and we played gin rummy and I read the Donald Duck comics in Danish, which she kept in a box in the basement.

I wrote back to Mom and asked her to tell Grandma I sent my love but otherwise trusted what she told me about the doctors' optimism. Needless to say, she asked about my plans in passing, because, naturally, she and my father weren't too pleased with my decision to quit university, and even less so with what I was employed doing instead. I told her I felt happy and was contemplating my future, as she and Dad had suggested.

I told Miko about my grandmother and was slightly taken aback when she responded by firing questions at me. We had never talked much about my family, and all of a sudden she was asking me not only about my grandmother but also about my parents, my brother, Mundi, life in Iceland, the weather, the dark winters, the mountains, the economy, transportation. In that manner, barely pausing between questions, slightly frenzied, I thought. I did my best to reply, but tried to conceal the hope her questions aroused in me of a possible future together, although I wasn't quite sure how to respond when she asked how it was for foreigners to live in Iceland. Were there many of them? Which countries did they come from? Was Icelandic difficult to learn? Did many Icelanders speak English? And so on.

At the same time, she became more careless, or relaxed, perhaps. She held my hand on the street and, a few days after the series of questions, kissed me when we met at a café, said to me one afternoon when we had made love in my room and she was on her way out: "Don't you think she knows what we are doing here?"

She had always been used to asking me to take a look outside to make sure Mrs. Ellis wasn't around before we dashed out of the house, but now she didn't let it bother her at all. "This is your room, after all," she said.

This change of heart seemed a bit sudden, but I never thought to question her about it. I enjoyed no longer having to be constantly on the lookout, feeling instead that we could be ourselves whether alone or with her university friends, Elizabeth and Penny, William and Patricia, all of whom (excepting Elizabeth, of course) seemed astonished when she introduced me to them. This was at the cinema, and Penny, who evidently spoke for all of them, exclaimed: "Where have you been hiding him?"

Now every day was like our weekend in Bath; every day it was sunny regardless. I felt happy when I woke up and happy when I went to sleep. When she wasn't with me, I missed her, and when I was with her, I dreaded her departure.

"This is my boyfriend, Kristófer."

That was how she introduced me. Simply and with that brightness in her voice.

It was only at Nippon where nothing much changed. Admittedly she would brush up against me when the two of us were alone in the kitchen but nothing more. It didn't happen often and the contact was fleeting. For my part, I was less daring and remained careful not to look at her in a way that might draw attention.

After this had been going on for over a fortnight, and I felt confident she wasn't about to change her behavior again, I allowed myself to talk to her about her father. We had attended an evening lecture with her friends and gone to a café after but were now at my place, where she was staying the night. I had been about to broach the subject of Takahashi-san since we'd left her friends but had gotten cold feet. When we were in bed with the lights out, I finally plucked up the courage.

"Miko . . ."

"Yes?"

"Are you asleep?"

"Yes."

Silence.

"What is it?"

"Nothing . . ."

"Come on, what is it?"

"Takahashi-san . . ." Just saying his name caused my heart to miss a beat. I broke off and lay there waiting. I instantly regretted opening my mouth.

I needn't have. She felt for my hand beneath the covers and said encouragingly: "Don't worry. I'm dealing with it."

"You are?"

"Yes."

"I don't want you to . . ."

"Don't worry."

I had the impression she was going to add something, something that would explain this change in her, but she remained silent.

"I love you," I said.

"I love you too," she said.

During the following week, two things happened that stand

out in my memory because they both made me happy. Grandma was discharged from hospital on Tuesday, and Takahashi-san told me Steve would be away over the weekend and asked if I could step in for him. Regarding Grandma, the doctors said she was on the mend after successful treatment, and although Takahashi-san didn't soliloquize about my abilities, he made it clear he had faith in me.

When he clapped me on the back, it flashed through my mind that Miko might have told him something about us. Not everything, surely, but enough, and that he had not been unhappy about it.

On Friday he had an appointment at the optician after lunch, so I stayed at the restaurant to prep for dinner. I was alone in the kitchen when Miko appeared shortly before four o'clock.

"Where is everybody?" she asked.

I explained.

She took up a position in the kitchen and watched me while I worked. I remember I was slicing vegetables. I also remember thinking how loud the knife sounded on the chopping board.

"Takahashi-san—" I began to say.

"What about him?"

"Did you say something to him?"

I glanced about instinctively, although I knew we were alone, as though afraid somebody was lurking or that the walls had ears.

"Come with me," she said, tugging my shirt.

"Where?"

"Come with me."

She pulled me into the pantry and kissed me. I was ill at ease.

"Somebody might come," I said.

"Nobody will come," she said, and started to undress. When I hesitated, she undid my belt and then wrapped herself around me.

I felt uncomfortable but tried not to let it show. It was as if

I were defiling a sacred place, and I kept thinking I could hear somebody coming in. When it was over, I got dressed in a hurry and was soon back chopping vegetables.

Miko disappeared into the bathroom. Just as she emerged, the door opened and Takahashi-san walked in. I remember being struck by the cheery greeting she gave him.

The owner of the flat was paying me a visit. He naturally had a key, but showed me the courtesy of ringing the door phone to ask if it was convenient for him to drop in.

The reason he had come was twofold. First, he wanted to welcome me and ask if I had everything I needed, and second, he had brought me some face masks which he thought might come in handy.

"You arrived just in time," he said. "Visitors from Iceland are now included in the travel ban." He hung the bag containing the face masks on the door handle. "Twenty masks," he said. "They can be difficult to find these days."

He himself wore a mask, so I couldn't see his face properly, but I would say he is in his mid-thirties. He speaks good English and is neat, in keeping with his flat. I told him he was very kind and offered to reimburse him for the masks, but he wouldn't hear of it.

"Welcome to Hiroshima," he said. "Don't hesitate to let me know if I can be of any assistance."

In the bag was also a tiny bottle of hand sanitizer, smaller than the ones in the flat, pocket-size. Indeed, it is in my jacket now, a mask is on my face, and I am holding a bouquet of flowers as I walk along the river at dusk. The bouquet is bigger than I had envisioned because the woman at the florist was so helpful that I felt bad asking her to make it smaller after she had gone to so much trouble putting it together.

I must confess that I felt a little hungover today after my evening with Kutaragi-san. This accounts for my melancholy and reminds me why I avoid alcohol. But I am feeling better now, especially after I ate some *okonomiyaki* at a food stall by the river and drank a glass of sparkling water. A great deal better, in fact, and I can think back warmly to Kutaragi-san's sake lesson and the Japanese whiskey we drank before our karaoke session. A trade-off, as Mundi refers to hangovers. Although he claims to be immune, naturally.

Miko was always a bit of a night owl, which is why I decided to visit her now, even though it's after eight o'clock. Thanks to Gunnar's research, I know which flat is hers and will turn back if I see that the lights are out. In one of her messages, she told me the virus has disrupted her sleeping patterns; she sometimes sleeps during the day, other times at night, and she's perpetually tired. "Occasionally I open my eyes and think I am in London." She didn't say anything else, but it was enough to get me thinking.

I find I have slowed my pace without realizing it. Having turned away from the river, I am now a stone's throw from her house. And yet I don't quite come to a halt and have stopped puzzling over what to say to her when we meet, stopped trying to find words that will bridge half a century.

The last corner. The building stands before me, a shade darker than in the photograph Gunnar showed me. But that was taken in broad daylight, and in addition, there are no streetlamps directly in front of the building. There is one up the street and another one slightly down the street, but they don't cast much light on the building itself.

I draw closer, pausing across the street as I look up at the windows on the second floor. A pair of pale curtains are partially drawn across two of them, and I think I see a faint light inside but then realize it's the streetlamps reflecting on the glass.

I wait. On the fourth floor, a woman holding a cloth in her hand walks past her window. She doesn't look out and seems to be talking to somebody who is perhaps sitting behind her at a kitchen table. She nods, puts down the cloth, then disappears. In a window on the third floor, a television screen flickers intermittently pale blue. Nothing more.

After a while I walk across the street to the entrance. Beside each door buzzer, you can read the residents' names. Only their surnames, apart from hers: Miko Nakamura, 2B. I recall the first time I wrote "Miko" in Japanese. It was in a book about Iceland that I gave her, a book of photographs I came across in a second-hand store. It was after she had asked me all about Iceland, the people, the mountains and modes of transport, the language. We were in a café. She opened the book, then closed it again.

Her lights are out, so I won't trouble her now. Hopefully she is sleeping. I am not worried about the flowers; they will survive overnight. Coincidentally, I saw a vase in one of the kitchen drawers I opened earlier, blue with yellow polka dots. It may be a little on the small side, in which case I shall simply remove some of those surplus tulips.

I sensed a slight impatience in Mrs. Ellis's voice that made me think she had been knocking on the door for some time. "Kristófer, Kristófer, are you there? You have a visitor . . ."

It took me a while to get my bearings, but I finally answered her and pulled on some clothes. It was eight o'clock. I had fallen asleep late and slept in, tired after a long day at work.

Of course, Mrs. Ellis had seen Miko come and go, and yet the two of them had never spoken. Nor had I introduced them, so I had only myself to blame if Mrs. Ellis behaved as though she didn't know Miko that morning.

In any event, I went downstairs to greet Miko in the hall-way, and we came back up to my room together. I was expecting her to say something sarcastic about my landlady after I had closed the door, but she was preoccupied. She reached into her bag and handed me a small package wrapped in old newspaper. I contemplated it in my hands but was too baffled to start un-wrapping it.

"I decided to stop by on my way to class," she said. "It's fragile."

Where I lived was nowhere near her university. She would have taken two buses and then walked over ten minutes. I said nothing but loosened the string around the package and peeled the newspaper away from the cup, which has since followed me everywhere—with its picture of a squirrel or a bird, possibly an owl.

And yet I didn't know what to say about the cup, which I thought was pretty, for I couldn't understand the urgency that had caused her to make this detour early in the morning. As the silence became awkward, my eye alighted on an article in the piece of newspaper which she had wrapped around the cup. "The Beatles at Tittenhurst Park" was the headline above a huge photograph of John Lennon and Yoko Ono. On the opposite page were other pictures of the Fab Four, taken mostly outside the country house Lennon and Ono had purchased recently. Lennon wore a wide-brimmed hat, a full beard, and had let his hair grow below his shoulders.

"Look," I said.

She glanced at the paper, then pushed it aside. Not aggressively but as she might discard something that was in her way. "This was my mom's cup," she said. "Dad gave it to me when I was little. I want you to have it now."

I took her in my arms and was about to say something when she wriggled free and picked up her bag. "I'll be late."

I followed her down the stairs, but before I could catch up, she had opened the door. I called after her, some words of farewell, but she barely looked back, then hurried down the street.

That was on Thursday. The next day she didn't arrive at work until just before six and left as soon as we closed. Before saying goodbye, she informed me that she wouldn't be coming in the next day because she and Takahashi-san were leaving town to visit some family friends. I use the verb "inform" purposefully, because her voice was oddly formal

"Where are you going?" I asked.

"To Brighton," she said.

"Thanks for the cup," I had time to say before she rushed off. The words sounded weird. She gave me a quick glance and then vanished.

Steve cooked on Saturday, and I assisted him. Hitomi waited tables. There wasn't much to do, not on Sunday either. This was the first time Takahashi-san had been away since I started working at Nippon. The place felt empty without him.

I went over that weekend in my head so many times, trying especially to see Hitomi before me, for I felt certain she must have known what was going on. And yet I could find no proof in what I remembered of her behavior, which was no different than usual. She scolded me and Steve, in jest, needless to say, complained the food was so badly plated she was embarrassed to serve it, said she would have to make sure the customers didn't see inside the kitchen, as they would faint from shock.

"*Gaijin* don't know how to cook Japanese food," she said.

"Go to hell," Steve said.

No. I couldn't see any signs. Not when I imagined Hitomi before me. But they screamed out at me when I thought about the morning Miko brought me the cup or my last exchange with Takahashi-san.

That was on the Monday. Mom and Dad had called that morning to tell me Grandma had died in the night. She had taken ill in the evening and passed away a few hours later.

"She asked about you," Mom said. "You were always her favorite."

We agreed I would travel home for her funeral.

"It would be good if you could come sooner rather than later," Dad said. "There's a lot to arrange."

I went over to Nippon in the early afternoon. Takahashi-san had popped out, so I sat and waited in the backyard. When he appeared a little later, I asked if I could take some leave. He walked straight up to me and shook my hand. I didn't recall him ever having done that before.

"Safe journey, Kristófer," he said. "Take care of yourself."

He gripped my hand and looked me straight in the eye. I had no idea that he was saying goodbye to me for the very last time.

Before I left, he said that Miko was still in Brighton. He was in the kitchen then, with his back half turned to me, so I didn't get the impression he was speaking directly to me. But he was, very specifically, although to this day I cannot figure out what was going on in his mind.

I booked my flight for Wednesday. I traveled light—even more so than on this trip. A suit and tie, a white shirt, my best shoes. And the cup, to have something to remember her by, for I realized I didn't have a single photograph of her, much less of the two us.

The flowers look fine this morning. The bouquet did fit in the vase, but given the opportunity, I decided to reduce it and have placed two tulips in a tall glass on the kitchen table. It looks better now, exactly the way I imagined it in the first place.

I ring the door phone a second time. It is almost nine in the morning. I rose at seven after a good night's sleep and was out of the house a little over an hour later. Before leaving, I checked Facebook, but there was nothing to see; she is as silent as the grave.

There is no reply. I switch the flowers from my right hand to my left, shift from one foot to the other, take a few steps back on the pavement, and look up at the front of the building. The curtains remain drawn, as they were last night, and there is no movement inside. In the kitchen on the fourth floor where the woman holding the cloth stood last night, a young boy looks out the window. I guess he is about ten, at most. He doesn't appear to be watching anything in particular.

I sit on a bench in the square across the street. "Square" is probably too grand a word, as all that's here is a round flower bed, the bench I am occupying, and a tiny memorial, dedicated to what I don't know.

I set down the flowers. There is some traffic on the street, more delivery vans than passenger vehicles, a few pedestrians on their way to work or to the grocery store on the corner. Almost everybody is wearing a face mask; this has changed since I was in Tokyo. I reach into my pocket and put mine on.

I have nothing better to do than sit here and watch the building across the street. I am somewhat at a loss but strangely calm. I guess I have always realized I might be clutching at straws, half expecting an empty house since she stopped replying to my messages. Maybe she has recovered; maybe she has reconsidered her position now that the emergency may be over, no longer sees any point in reconnecting with her past. It would be perfectly understandable, people think differently when they believe they are close to dying, they feel a need to settle things before it's too late, give or ask for explanations, tie up loose ends. One day I may be in those shoes myself.

I hope this is what has happened. That she has recovered and gone away somewhere to avoid seeing me. I prefer not to contemplate the other possible explanations for her silence.

It is eighteen degrees outside, and although the sun isn't shining, I feel warm here on the bench wearing only a shirt under my blue windbreaker. I have resolved to wait until a neighbor appears, on the way into or out of the building. I am even prepared in case I need to make myself understood in Japanese, having this morning jotted down a few phrases with the help of my dictionary and an online translation tool.

I leave the bouquet on the bench while I try to find something to eat. I skipped breakfast this morning, so I am feeling rather peckish. Farther along the street is a food cart, positioned at such an angle that I can see parts of the building while I wait for my coffee and pastry. Not the main entrance, however, which is why I can't relax until I walk back to the bench with my breakfast.

Ten o'clock arrives, then eleven o'clock. I am keeping a close eye on the fourth floor where I saw the woman last night and the boy this morning, but they haven't made another appearance, any more than the other residents. It occurs to me they might have gone out while I was buying my coffee, and I regret not staying put. But then I remind myself that I have nothing better to do than sit here enjoying the fine weather, and if they did go out, they will have to come back. In addition, the sun is showing itself every now and then and will soon start shining here in the square, if I am not mistaken.

It's one thing to be an optimist and quite another to deceive oneself. The longer I stare up at those windows, the less able I am to avoid confronting the fact that something bad might have happened. Nowhere in her messages did she say she was getting better, and despite her bravado and talk of being "ridiculously weak and lazy," it was evident that the virus had its claws in her.

I arrived too late. After all these years, I arrived a few days too late.

A sudden anguish takes hold of me, and I leap to my feet. Before I know it, I have crossed the street. I press the door phone again, I wait, I listen to the silence.

There are many kinds of silence. Mostly it calms the mind. Sometimes it brims with expectation. But this is the same silence that greeted me when I came back from Iceland after Grandma's funeral to find Nippon empty and abandoned. This is a death-like silence.

I sit down again and pick up the bouquet, which has somehow shrunk and lost the harmony I thought I had achieved when I trimmed it this morning. It looks as if it's beginning to wilt in the heat.

We are in the midst of a global pandemic. I closed my restaurant and traveled halfway across the world. What for? To get
back what never existed? To make myself feel better—to search
for something that will justify how I have lived my life?

The sun is edging its way into the square and has almost
reached the bench when I notice a woman walking toward the
entrance across the street. She is wearing a pale coat and pulling
a shopping cart behind her. She doesn't seem in any great hurry
and stops to look at her phone before reaching into her pocket
for a key. At that point I leap to my feet and run across the street.

I reach her before she has opened the door. She gives a little
start and I quickly apologize. It is strange talking with a face
mask on—my voice sounds deeper and a bit muffled—but I don't
feel I can take it off. She is wearing a mask too, and I can see
from her eyes that she is more curious than alarmed.

I explain the purpose of my visit. In English to start, but
when she seems not to understand, I reach for my piece of paper
and tell her in broken Japanese that I am looking for Miko Nakamura. She contemplates me in silence and looks at the piece
of paper in my hand. Then she asks in English: "What is your
name?"

I tell her. She frowns, so I take my pen out of my pocket and
write it down on the piece of paper.

"I heard what you said," she says.

I put the pen back in my pocket. "Do you know her?" I ask.

She doesn't reply but glances at the bouquet in my hand.

"They need water," I say.

Prelude, a prayer, hymns, the scriptures. A solo, a gospel. The tribute—Klara Jónsdóttir was born at Hvammur Farm on the fourteenth of May 1885 . . .

I tried to concentrate on what the priest was saying but struggled to keep my thoughts from straying. "Klara was a generous hostess. Her grandchildren loved visiting her on Hávallagata, where there were pancakes and hot chocolate, often with whipped cream, waiting for them . . ." He mentioned the Donald Duck comics, Grandma's charity work, her trip to Norway to visit her sister in 1951. Her needlework and her love of singing . . . But I was thinking about Miko. No matter how hard I tried, I couldn't stop thinking about her. The look on her face when she contemplated something. Our weekend in Bath when we got caught in the rain. The evening when I asked her why Takahashi-san mustn't know about us and she slipped her hand beneath the covers and held me and wouldn't let me close my eyes. Those moments and others like them.

I felt ashamed and tried to thrust aside these images that had captured my thoughts and to think instead of Grandma, who didn't warrant this disrespect, who deserved nothing less than for me to celebrate her with all my heart and to nod in agreement when the priest reminded us how much she had given us.

I couldn't wait to leave the country. My parents sensed my unease. "Is something the matter?" Mom asked.

"No," I replied.

Dad asked Mundi and me to help him clear out the flat on Hávallagata, as he had decided to sell it. My return flight to London was booked for Saturday, and he asked if I could put off traveling until after the weekend. I couldn't refuse but was on the brink of making up some excuse to be able to leave.

We made good progress. I was keen to get it finished, and my eagerness got on Mundi's nerves. "Are you in a hurry or something?" he asked, and was evidently speaking for both himself and my father, although Dad was silent and commented only when he noticed I had thrown away the Donald Duck comics. I told him the truth, which was that I had put them in the garbage by accident. For a brief moment he looked at me as if he didn't recognize me, and then we resumed working. When I said goodbye to them at the bus station twelve days after my arrival, I had the impression he and Mom were worried. But they did their best not to let it show.

The next morning I waited for Miko outside the lab building where she worked. I knew she always arrived at the last minute, but I was there at twenty to nine, as I was up early and couldn't wait to see her.

When it was half past nine and she hadn't appeared, I assumed she must have started early that day. Obviously I was disappointed, but I didn't give up hope. Not even after I went back later that day, when she was supposed to be getting out of work, and drew a blank then as well.

Before Grandma passed away, I had promised Mrs. Ellis to fix the kitchen cupboard doors, as some of the hinges and handles had come loose. It wasn't difficult, but it took me until midnight. I set my alarm before I went to sleep, and by eight o'clock the following morning, I was waiting in the same place as the day before.

I needn't describe the outcome of that expedition; indeed, I have given it scarcely any thought during my decades-long reliving of that day. It was simply the opening note, a harmless drifting chord that didn't appear to herald anything of importance, certainly not the deafening silence that awaited me when I made my way to Nippon and that has been ringing in my ears ever since.

I don't know why I went there that morning. I hadn't yet started to worry, although I certainly found it strange that Miko hadn't shown up at the lab two days in a row. Maybe I thought she'd had to fill in for somebody at the restaurant; maybe I wanted to drop by because I missed the kitchen, though I wasn't expected there until the day after; maybe I wanted to see if Takahashi-san had slipped a haiku in the pot while I was away.

Such was my innocence that I couldn't make sense of what the sign on the door said. "CLOSED." Until lunch? For the rest of the week? Until next month? I knew the sign, it was kept in the broom closet, but I didn't remember ever seeing it on the door. I didn't have my key on me but instinctively tried the door handle, without success. When I peered through the windows, I saw nothing out of the ordinary at first; the tables and chairs were where they were supposed to be, the desk in reception, the hangers on the rail by the door, nothing out of the ordinary until I noticed the pot was missing. Then I leaned closer, cupping my hands to shield my eyes from the morning light, pressed my face against the cold glass, and realized that everything but the fixtures and furniture had vanished, the shelves behind the bar were empty, bottles and glasses gone, the pictures on the walls nowhere to be seen.

However hard I've tried, however long I've spent racking my brain, beating my head against the wall, laying siege to my memory in the still of night, storming it in broad daylight, I've never managed to retrieve a single fragment of the seconds that followed, the minutes that followed, not even the next quarter of an hour. No shred of an image, no echo of a sound. Nothing. Until I was running home to fetch the key, sweating profusely, gasping for breath, and drained of strength the way one is sometimes when fleeing in a bad dream.

When at last I unlocked the door to Nippon, I was met by an emptiness so devastating that I felt as if I had walked into a wall when I stepped into the semi-darkness. Everything had vanished from the kitchen, the bar, the pantry, and the bathroom, every loose object, every trace of the people who had spent such a big part of their lives there for years and years. I wandered around for a few minutes, so emptied out and numb I could barely look inside the cupboards and drawers, and soon gave up and just stood still in the kitchen—holding my knife, which had been left for me on the table where I usually worked.

There was no note with it. There was no need for one. On its own in the middle of the table, a tea towel wrapped around the blade, the handle protruding. Beside it was an envelope containing the wages Takahashi-san owed me. Even though I was too devastated to acknowledge it to myself, I think that day I knew I was never going to see them again.

A storm blows a ship off course, waves wash driftwood onto the shore. Another day rises, another evening puts an end to it. Autumn comes, then winter. Nature has its way, and in the stillness of night, the moon shines on ebony hair, leaving behind a silver thread that glitters in memory decades later.

I was twenty-three years old and had known her for just a few months when she disappeared. I had my whole life ahead of me, whether an untrodden path or a charted course, I believed I controlled that myself. I was an independent man who had defied convention and common sense by quitting university. I had gone to sea, stood out on deck, and gazed up at the spheres amid a stillness so perfect it might have been the remains of the silence that reigned before the world began. I had long hair and a beard; I wore round glasses. Mom told me I had been strong-willed from the beginning and that I seldom cried.

Minutes become hours and a moment becomes an eternity. I am seventy-five years old, sitting on this bench feeding two little birds crumbs from the pastry I bought with my coffee. I am thinking about the knife on the table, my teacup, moonlight on raven hair. It's as if time has stood still, as if nothing has happened in the half century that has passed.

The woman said nothing when I apologized for the state of the flowers but instead inserted the key into the lock and vanished inside the building. She didn't ask me to wait, but she didn't send me away either. I feel this bodes well and yet I curb my optimism.

I look up at the windows, which are as oblivious as before to what is happening out here on the street. I think I see movement behind one of them, but afterward there is nothing. In the kitchen on the fourth floor, a man looks out. He is wearing a face mask. This strikes me as odd, but I comprehend when, soon afterward, he emerges from the house accompanied by the boy and the woman with the tea towel.

I had never been to Miko and Takahashi-san's house, but later that day I had made my way to their little street in Hampstead after having stopped off at home with the knife, as I couldn't be carrying it around with me. It was a wild-goose chase, although I found out from a woman who lived in their building that they had recently moved out, "three or four days ago," possibly five, she wasn't exactly sure. Where they went, she had no idea.

"I only saw him," the woman said. "The father. Not the girl."

I discovered how little I knew about my fellow workers. Over the next few days, I tried in vain to locate Hitomi and Goto-san. It was only some months later that I came across Hitomi at a Japanese restaurant that had just opened in Kensington. She was as friendly as ever but couldn't explain Miko and Takahashi-san's disappearance and said she suspected it might have been health-related. "Not that Takahashi-san ever said anything to me or to Goto-san. He never spoke about himself."

She told me he had been generous to them, paid them several months' salary. "Until the end of the year," she said. "Goto-san used it to buy a ticket home. He isn't back yet. Maybe he will never come back."

"What about Takahashi-san and Miko?" I asked. Did she know where they had gone?

She shook her head.

"To Japan?"

"He didn't say where they were going," she said.

"What about Miko?" What had she said?

"She wasn't there the last few days," said Hitomi. "I was sad not to be able to say goodbye to her. But it happened so quickly."

I tried to squeeze more information out of her, but she didn't have much to say. She did mention more than once that Takahashi-san hadn't been himself the last few days, he was subdued and oddly frail.

"I said to Goto-san I felt he had aged several years in a few days," she said. "Suddenly he was like an old man."

"When did he start preparing to close?" I asked her.

"When did you go to Iceland for your grandma's funeral?" she asked me.

I told her.

"On the Wednesday?"

"Yes."

"I think he spoke to us on Thursday. And Saturday was the last day we were open."

"Did Miko work that day?"

"No, only Goto-san and the guy who covered for you. Takahashi-san had already given Steve his notice."

I asked if the regular customers had come to say goodbye.

"No. Takahashi-san didn't tell anyone he was closing."

I got no more out of her despite my continued probing. It was late afternoon and I had waited until she took her break. Before I said goodbye, I asked her to let me know if she heard anything. I was working at a restaurant near Covent Garden then and wrote down the name for her on a piece of paper.

"I doubt I will," she said, then added: "Didn't he pay you?"

Yes, he had paid me, I told her.

The bouquet of flowers is so wilted, I consider discarding it. But there is no real hurry, and I have seen cut flowers in a sorrier state perk up when put in water. It is lying beside me on the bench, on my right, and I switch it to my left, where the sun is now shining. Not because I think the sun's rays will revive it, but at least the light should enhance the colors.

This maneuver doesn't take long, and yet when I look up again, I see the woman standing in the entrance across the street, waving to me. Her body language suggests she has been there for a few moments, at least, and is growing impatient. I leap to my feet and hurry over to her, remembering at the last moment to bring the bouquet with me.

I didn't connect the word *hibakusha* with their disappearance, not even after I came across the article in *The Guardian*. That was in mid-October. I cut it out and read it over and over, and afterward I thought I understood why Takahashi-san had abandoned his country when he did, packed up and gone abroad with a very young Miko, speaking no language other than his own, knowing no place other than his hometown.

The author was Graham Tucker, a young journalist I had noticed before because he had a lively, original style, whether he was writing about the Woodstock Festival or Neil Armstrong and his fellow astronauts' trip to the moon. Tucker was inspired to write the article by an interview he did with a doctor in Hamburg (I don't remember what Tucker was doing there) who had worked with international organizations in Japan, primarily in Hiroshima and Nagasaki, researching the effects of the atomic bombs on the health of survivors.

Hibakusha. In the piece, the word appeared early on. Tucker explained briefly which group of people had been given this name, described the injuries and the diseases they struggled with, before turning to the focus of the piece: the prejudice these folks had to endure in their own country. Few appeared using their real name, but they described the day the bombs fell, the following days and weeks, the compassion that slowly gave way to prejudice. People began to treat them as if they were contagious—like lepers. Children were refused permission to attend schools, would-be brides and grooms abandoned their fiancés upon learning they were *hibakusha*, some people lost their jobs, others were unable to rent properties. A shop owner in Tokyo had to close his business after a customer discovered where he came from and word got around. And yet the attack had taken place nearly twenty years before. Many people attempted to hide their past; they moved away, started over.

I was particularly interested in an interview with a woman who was pregnant and living in Hiroshima when the bomb fell. Four months later she gave birth to a healthy baby, having escaped herself with nothing more than slight radiation poisoning. And yet both she and her child became outcasts. They moved away when her son was a year old, she didn't want to say where. She had changed her name, and although her son was now a grown man, she hadn't told him the truth about his past. She doubted she ever would.

"Yet I'm still a *hibakusha*," Miko had said that night in Bath. Now I understood what she had meant.

I felt as if I had solved some mystery, even if it cast light only on the past. Takahashi-san had achieved his aim, he had escaped prejudice, built a new and better life for himself and for Miko. I didn't doubt that the past had taken its toll on them both, especially on Takahashi-san, who had been forced to bear the burden of it alone, incapable of sharing it with others, unlikely to ask for support, as they call it nowadays, assuming there was any on offer.

And yet the article aroused in me a feeling of hope, at least for a while. I concluded that it was almost unthinkable for them to have returned to Japan, not after everything that had happened there, and I focused my search instead on the few places in England I remembered Miko mentioning. For example, the small Devon towns of Woolacombe, Salcombe, and Torquay, where Takahashi-san had taken her for short summer holidays when she was younger, Bristol and Birmingham, and Edinburgh in Scotland. And of course Brighton, where she'd said she and Takahashi-san were going to visit family friends the weekend before I flew to Iceland for Grandma's funeral.

During the following weeks and months, I went to all those places. First Brighton, then Bristol and Birmingham, then Edinburgh, and finally the coastal towns in Devon. And there my search ended one Sunday in October when the tourists were long gone, the beaches deserted, a cold breeze sweeping in off the sea. There is nothing quite as bleak as a seaside resort in winter, the interminable gray skies, the silence broken only by an occasional seagull's squawk and the whistling wind, the good times over and the promise of warm weather such a distant prospect that contemplating it only makes you feel worse. It began to rain as I stood outside a whitewashed restaurant with boarded-up windows, gazing out to sea at a container ship far from the shore and moving slowly into the distance. I didn't hurry to leave but stood still until the ship was out of sight, swallowed up by the rain and fog. By that time I was completely soaked through.

I worked as a kitchen assistant at a restaurant in Covent Garden until the spring. The food wasn't bad and the prices were reasonable. The chef was French, as was the menu—*escargots, croque monsieur, coq au vin, bouillabaisse, beef bourguignon*. He wasn't a bad cook, but he was lazy and slapdash. As for me, I kept myself to myself, and in any case, my mind was elsewhere.

I hardly socialized but kept in touch with Miko's friend

Elizabeth to check if she had heard from her. She never did and maintained that she was as surprised as I by their sudden departure. I was foolish enough to mistrust her at first. It wasn't fair, but I couldn't help myself.

Occasionally I would make my way to Nippon. Usually in the evenings. The place was still standing empty when I left to return to Iceland, with no sign of any new tenants about to move in. Once or twice I went to the house in Hampstead but only felt worse afterward.

Finally I gave up. My parents sensed something was wrong, and when Dad announced he was coming over, I decided to preempt him. I left my job at the French restaurant and my room at Mrs. Ellis's, packed my books and knickknacks into a box, and flew home on my mom's birthday, June 4, 1970.

It was sunny that day, hardly a cloud on the horizon. One year before, almost to the day, I had cooked breakfast for Miko, held her in my arms for the first time, clasped her tight. I watched the city dwindle, the houses shrink and merge into a gray expanse, the river disappear. This was where we had enjoyed our few moments together, where I had found a happiness I never knew existed, intense happiness and then grief.

Maybe I believed I was leaving behind the city and everything associated with it, maybe I thought that with time I could start over again. But she followed me like the books I packed into the box and the teacup I kept hold of on the plane, the one I left on the kitchen table this morning. The city and its memories, the joy, the sorrows, and the anger—and the love that has stood in the way of so much all these years.

She is waiting for me in the half-open doorway, and I think she is going to usher me inside. Instead she asks me to stand still on the sidewalk in front of her, raises her phone, and before I know it, she has taken a picture of me.

"Wait there," she says, closing the door behind her.

I am not quite sure how to react, but I don't need to think about it long, because I feel a wave of optimism course through me. It starts in the pit of my stomach and flows into my arms and fingertips and up to my head, penetrating deep inside. Miko, I say to myself, this was her idea. Only she could think up such a thing.

The woman isn't gone for more than five minutes. This time she invites me in, but instead of heading for the stairs when the door closes, she pauses in the hallway. "Nakamura-san has been ill," she says.

I tell her I am aware of this.

"She came home from the hospital only yesterday."

"Was she in the hospital again?" I say.

"Yes, she has been very ill."

"And now?"

"Very tired."

"But not ill?"

She doesn't reply but finally mounts the stairs. She doesn't say anything, but I assume she expects me to follow her. She doesn't look over her shoulder and moves slowly, even though she is oddly light on her feet, walking almost on tiptoe, painfully slowly, until we reach the second floor. There she stops, indicates a tiny corridor with a door at the end, ajar, and a chair outside. "Sit there," she says.

"What?" I ask.

"She doesn't want to talk to you on the phone."

She goes away, and I wait until I hear the door downstairs close. Only then do I edge my way along the corridor, one step at a time, amid a dense silence. The overhead lights aren't on, but a faint glow emanates from the crack in the door.

I come to a halt a couple of meters from the chair. It's no more than three or four steps, and yet suddenly it seems like such a yawning gulf that I haven't the strength to continue. Only for a moment, though, then I slowly manage to silence the voice of despair that has been growing louder these past few days, ruthlessly making itself heard at every opportunity. Little by little I raise my eyes from my shoes and move first my left foot and then my right, small steps toward a precise goal: the white kitchen chair turned at an angle so that, instead of the crack in the door, I will be facing a white wall with a photograph from London—a scene from Westminster, to be precise.

I sit down and look at the picture as I listen for a sound from within the flat. But I hear nothing, no coughs or sighs, much less footsteps, only the hissing sound in my head. I am on tenterhooks and finally can't help breaking the silence. "Miko?"

Her name echoes for an instant, and then silence descends once more on the narrow corridor. Deep silence until I hear a voice from the other side of the door: "I've never seen you without a beard."

I am so overwhelmed that I can't speak. It's as if her voice is coming from inside me, from inside my head, where I have been hearing it for the past fifty years. Then I feel astonished at how little this voice has changed, neither deepened nor grown fainter, not lost its mocking quality or the charm that immediately sets something aflutter in my chest. Naturally she is weaker than I remember and, even if she tries not to let it show, a little frailer.

"I shaved it off a long time ago," I say.

It dawns on me that I am utterly unprepared. I have never thought about what I might say to her if I had the opportunity, never composed any words in my head, let alone on paper, though it would have been most sensible.

"Forty years ago, I think," I add, "and by then I had already started trimming it."

Silence.

"Have you had a good life, Kristófer?"

My heart leaps. Not because of her question but, rather, when I hear her say my name.

"I can't complain," I say.

"I recognized you immediately," she says quickly. "From the picture Keiko took. Hashimoto-san . . . Although she's not a very good photographer."

"Why?"

"I can see more of the street than of you."

"She took it in a hurry," I say.

"I wanted to see what you looked like."

"I haven't changed a bit." I see her before me, half smiling.

"Where are you staying?"

I tell her. She asks about the flat. I say it's a decent size, bright and clean. "I have everything I need," I say. "And it's only a short walk away."

Silence.

"I wrote you a letter once. I even found your address, but when I reached the post office, I got cold feet."

"Miko," I say, "there's no hurry . . ."

"The doctors thought I was going to die. Otherwise I wouldn't have troubled you."

"You haven't troubled me."

"These doctors, you can't trust them."

"How right you are."

Silence.

"Kristófer . . ."

"Yes . . ."

"Forgive me."

"You needn't . . ."

"Forgive me."

Silence.

"I brought you some flowers."

"I saw them in the photograph. Keiko pointed them out to me."

"She didn't seem too impressed."

"The doctors say I'm no longer infectious, but I don't know if it's true."

"The flowers need to be put in water," I say.

She doesn't reply, but I can see from the light shining through the crack in the door onto the white wall that she is moving.

I stand up. "Miko?"

"Yes . . ."

I pick up the chair and move it to the side. I straighten my shirt and switch the bouquet from my right hand to my left before grasping the door handle.

Slowly I push the door open. I hesitate, perhaps waiting for her to tell me to stop, then I clasp the handle once more.

She is standing in the doorway, having sat on a chair identical to mine but which she has now pushed aside. Daylight streams through the window behind her, enveloping her in its glow.

For an instant we look into each other's eyes. Then I breach the few steps separating us and enfold her in my arms, holding her close, as I did long ago. She clutches me with both arms too.

I say nothing, neither of us does, but the next thing I know, tears are streaming down my cheeks. I don't try to wipe them away, for I don't want to let go of her. I have cried twice in three days now. I didn't know I still could.

I don't know how long we stand there. But then gradually we loosen our hold and both wipe the tears from our faces. We smile.

I have let the bouquet drop to the floor, so I stoop to pick it up.

"We must rescue these flowers," she says, and we walk together hand in hand into the sunlit flat.

There is a lot to see here. The Peace Memorial Park and the Peace Memorial Museum, the castle, the shopping area on Miyajima, the temples and statues. The castle is illuminated at night, as is the Itsukushima Shrine, which stands in the water and appears to be floating on the gentle spring tides. They say it's an amazing sight, and many people, young and old, flock there after sundown to find peace and tranquility, which they undoubtedly try to carry with them and preserve as long as they can.

Despite Miko's exhortations and the attractions' proximity, I haven't visited any of them. I get up early, take a shower, shave, and then set off for her home, where I make breakfast for us. Sometimes I stop off on the way at the grocery shop or the bakery, sometimes I don't need to. I make coffee, I brew tea.

A week has gone by since I arrived. She still sleeps a lot,

though less than before. This morning we played cards; yesterday evening I put a record on the gramophone, some Japanese jazz she chose. We sat listening to it on the sofa. We held hands. On a small table next to the bookshelves, a lamp glowed.

She was exhausted after my arrival. I don't really know how she managed to get up that day and sit on the chair by the door talking to me until I finally pushed it open and walked in. Once we were in the kitchen, she showed me where to find a vase for the flowers. She had to lean against the kitchen table while I filled it with water, then she asked me to help her sit. I had to steady her in the chair. Soon after, I helped her into the bedroom, where she slept for the rest of the day. She slept most of the next day too.

During the first few days, she spoke very little. And when she did, I sometimes had the impression she was feverish. But then every once in a while, she would perk up and I would catch glimpses of her as I remembered her.

This has been happening more and more these past few days as her health improves. Hashimoto-san, who comes every day, agrees, and seems reconciled to my presence. At first she blamed me for Miko's frailty and told me my visit had made things worse.

Those were her words: "made things worse."

But her attitude has changed now. She is more friendly toward me and even chats with me when she stops by. She told me how she and Miko met, teaching English at the same school.

"We were the English Department," she said. "Miko and me. For twenty-eight years."

She is perhaps a little younger than Miko, single. She lives in the neighborhood with her dog. He is ten years old and his name is Hamlet.

For the first couple of nights, I slept in the sitting room.

Hashimoto-san was slightly taken aback when I greeted her the morning after my visit, and she looked questioningly at me. But she forgot all thoughts of me when I told her how poorly Miko was doing, went straight in to see her, and stayed with her for a good while. When she came out, I asked if she shouldn't call the doctor.

She called him the next day. Meanwhile I returned to my flat, jumped in the shower, and put on clean clothes. By the time I returned, the doctor had left.

"He said she may take a while to recover," explained Hashimoto-san. "It's the same for a lot of people. She's lucky to still be alive."

Yesterday Hashimoto-san and I went to the shops together. She had been cooking for Miko before I arrived, and I had the impression that she felt I was taking over from her. With that in mind, on my third day, I invited her to have dinner with us. She took Miko's food to her in bed and then sat down with me at the kitchen table. I think she enjoyed the meal.

I don't know what Miko has told her about us. Hashimoto-san hasn't said anything, and I haven't asked. That evening over dinner, after contemplating me as though seeing me for the first time, she said suddenly: "So you are the man . . ."

That was all.

Occasionally, when Miko calls out to me, I find her sleeping when I enter her room. This happens at any time of the day or night. Once she said: "Let's go to Kure." She was talking in her sleep then too.

We still haven't spoken about the past. She has made a few attempts, but when I see how tiring it is for her, I suggest we let it wait. "There's no hurry," I say.

Yesterday evening, when we were listening to the jazz in the living room, I thought she was going to start recollecting something when she spoke. It wasn't just what she said but the way she broke off mid-sentence: "I've been thinking—"

I wasn't ready yet for a conversation about our past, so I gave a little shudder but said nothing. Thankfully she had something else on her mind.

"Nakamura-san," she said. "He deserved better."

She didn't have to say any more. I was on the verge of mentioning Inga but refrained.

"He was a teacher, like me," she went on. "He taught math. He's a very meticulous man."

I was taken aback. "He's still alive?" I asked.

"Yes, we got divorced."

I tried to recall what she had said about her husband on Face-book, but all I could remember with any precision was that they were childless. When I checked afterward, I found no other mention of him in her messages. I had just assumed he'd passed away.

She said no more about him there on the sofa. I stood up to turn the record over. It gave me pleasure lifting the stylus and lowering it again, watching it move across the grooves. It's been years since I got rid of my old record player.

That evening when I went in to say good night to her, she mentioned her ex-husband again. She had turned out the light; I was leaving the room.

"Nakamura-san is a good man," she said softly. "We were divorced in ninety-seven. A month after Takahashi-san died."

That was all, and I pulled the door closed behind me.

I had asked her about her father on my first visit. She didn't say much, only that he had died over twenty years ago. Then she looked at me as if to acknowledge that we had much left to talk about.

There is a framed photograph of him on the sideboard in

the living room. It was taken by the sea; behind him are some small boats in a harbor. The sun is low in the sky and casts a golden glow on the boats, while Takahashi-san himself is in partial shade. Maybe that explains why he seems so very small that I find it quite impossible to reconcile him with the image I have been carrying of him in my head.

I sent Sonja a long message on Facebook yesterday describing the flat I am living in now, what I have seen of the city and what I have yet to see, the good weather I have been blessed with since my arrival, the cherry trees, which are now in full bloom. In particular I mentioned the Peace Memorial Museum, which I finally visited yesterday and I can't stop thinking about. I said this to Sonja but then edited my message before pressing send when I realized I had described what I'd witnessed in too much detail. Instead I limited myself to general comments about the atomic bomb and its effects, too general probably to convey much of anything.

"Otherwise, I'm fine," I wrote. "I like it here; the people are kind and considerate. I am trying to learn some of the language but it's going slowly. I keep myself occupied . . ."

I had intended to tell her something about my reasons for coming here, but I couldn't find the right words. I mentioned something about "friends" and then deleted it. Instead I asked how Villi and Axel were doing and said to send them my love.

Sonja and I were both with Inga when she passed away. It was after eleven o'clock at night. She had been going steadily down-hill for the past few days, and the nurses were expecting her to go at any time. She was heavily medicated and for the most part unconscious.

Just before she breathed her last, she came to briefly. Maybe for a minute, I am not quite sure. She whispered something, but it was difficult to hear. Sonja leaned over her. "I'm so proud of you," Inga managed to say.

I drew closer, taking care not to push Sonja out of the way. She was now sobbing continuously. Inga looked at me. She had difficulty keeping her eyes open, but I had the distinct impression she was trying to smile. "I know you did your best" was all she said.

She was only half conscious, so it would be foolish to make too much of what we thought we heard. I didn't use those exact words but said as much to Sonja. I realize now it had the opposite effect and might explain the tone of her obituary and her attitude toward me afterward. I probably have myself to blame.

In my Facebook message to Sonja, I certainly wanted to explain my trip here, to be honest with her. I wanted to describe to her how I feel. I wanted to tell her how happy I am. But I couldn't do it. It wouldn't be fair to her or to Inga. Maybe I never will.

She replied to me later that day, asked a few harmless questions I could easily answer, told me they were imposing tighter restrictions to combat the spread of the virus in Iceland, hospitalizations were on the rise, there were rumors of a shortage of masks and other personal protection equipment. Many of her clients were anxious. I could sense she was too, and I tried to give her some encouragement.

"It's surprising, though not strange when you think about

it," I wrote back, "that in this place where the atomic bomb fell, every memorial—museums, parks, monuments, and squares—is dedicated to peace. Nor is it strange that it permeates you."

I didn't say more, as I find it difficult to express how I feel without sounding like an evangelist. But Sonja had moved on to more pressing matters when she replied, so I needn't have worried.

"There's a ban on social gatherings, which means we can't celebrate Villi's birthday. Needless to say, he's terribly disappointed. I feel so bad for him."

Maybe it's a measure of how at ease I am that her words didn't cause me to have a knee-jerk reaction and start ranting to myself about her obsession with birthdays.

Nor do I let it upset me when Mundi texts me out of the blue. I have just shaved and am choosing which clothes to wear today. As usual, his tone is rather brusque. It's past midnight his time.

"How many times a day do you take a leak?" he asks.

I haven't heard from him since his nonsense about Baldur. For my part I have stuck by my decision to leave him alone for the remainder of my trip, or at least not to be the first one to get in touch.

"That depends how much liquid I drink," I reply.

"My stupid doctor wants me to piss sitting down, like a woman," he writes back immediately, with the usual keyboard errors.

Instead of letting his tone get my back up, I remind myself that Mundi, this overbearing hulk of a man, has always been terrified of doctors. "Don't you do that sometimes anyway?"

I doubt he finds this amusing. In any case, he doesn't reply immediately. Meanwhile I pull on my socks and trousers and remind myself of the conversation we had a year ago about urination and prostate trouble. Things were very busy at work when he called, and he took so long to get to the point that I had to tell him I didn't have time and would talk to him later. As I recall, he didn't call back.

"What about at night?" he writes.

"Once," I reply, and then to make him feel better: "Sometimes twice."

There is another pause before he replies, and when he finally does, he has taken more care, as the message contains no mistakes. "He wants to take a sample."

I do my best to be positive, assuring him that doctors like to be on the safe side. "He is just being thorough," I write.

"He's new," Mundi responds. "The old one never wanted samples."

I assume he isn't criticizing his former GP but, rather, indicating that the new one doesn't know what he's doing. But I sense his unease, and suddenly my heart goes out to my brother, alone in his retirement flat, his fellow residents dying of boredom, with nothing to do apart from listening to the radio and playing solitaire, his seafaring days long gone and little to look forward to other than tests and procedures performed on a body that once commanded ships' crews and was admired by men and women alike but is now a pale shadow of what it once was.

"I believe sitting helps the bladder empty more easily," I write, just for the sake of it. "Maybe I'll train myself to do it."

The conversation peters out. I put on my shirt and open the windows to air the room. I am starting to feel at home in this flat and have decided to contact the landlord later today. I don't suppose he has many bookings in the offing, but I want to make sure. Be on the safe side, like I said to Mundi.

I have also resolved to call Baldur. First I will talk to Frissi to see how he feels about renting the space to Baldur, for whom I will naturally provide glowing references. Having said this, I still have concerns about how he will cope with the stresses and strains of running a restaurant. But he is a grown man, and I don't wish to stand in his way. As for the fixtures and fittings, he can have those.

Before going out, I put on my mask, close the windows, and draw the curtains to prevent the flat from getting too hot when the sun comes out. Just as I am about to lock the door, I remember the box of chocolates I haven't yet given Miko. I go back to fetch it, studying it for a moment before putting it in a bag. Unfortunately I still can't place the mountain in the picture, although it looks even more familiar now than when I bought the box at the airport.

"Let's imagine it's daytime, I'm going to, anyway, and you and I are in your room. Or in the backyard at Nippon. It makes little difference, I've pictured us in both places, though more often in your room . . . We're alone and you start asking me about Takahashi-san. And I answer you. I don't try to change the subject. I don't cry. Or drag you into the pantry to wriggle out of giving you an answer . . . I tell you the truth."

It's late in the evening and we are sitting in her living room. She didn't want to turn the lights on as night fell, said she would find it easier to speak to me in the dark. "There's no hurry," I told her. But she is getting her strength back and says she can't wait any longer. She is becoming more herself again, wanting to sit here in the half-light and talk to me as if we were still that young couple sneaking into my room late one afternoon. As if time has stood still.

"I never pictured us having this conversation here . . ."

"We don't have to," I insist.

She looks straight ahead. I decide it's best if I do the same. My hands resting in my lap.

"Haven't you often hated me?"

I am startled. "No," I say.

"Never?"

"No. Never."

"I would have hated myself," she says.

A glimmer of light from the streetlamps seeps through the window but doesn't reach us. We hear a car drive by, stop, continue.

When she begins to talk, it's as if the words have been there all the time, a part of the silence, but now slowly detach themselves from it.

"I was ten when Dad first told me about what happened to Mom. About Hiroshima. Before that he never really spoke about the past. All I knew was that she had died when I was little and that they had lived in Kure. 'We are English now,' he used to say, 'that's all that matters.' Until my tenth birthday. That's when I first heard the word *hibakusha*.

"We were sitting at the kitchen table. He told me why we had left Japan. He spoke of the prejudices. Only he didn't use that word, because he himself believed them. He was afraid that inside me lurked imperfections that would reveal themselves in time. He told me I could never have children because they wouldn't be born healthy.

"I remember feeling frightened. I thought I was suffering from some terrible disease, that I was slowly dying. He consoled me and I vowed to obey all his orders. I had never seen him cry before.

"From then on, every birthday, he made me repeat my promise. Apart from that, he never mentioned the curse hanging over me. Until I started menstruating. Then he was like a man in the grip of some terrible anguish. I was thirteen.

"For the first few years his rules and prohibitions didn't affect me. But then I hit puberty. Boys started taking an interest in me. I started becoming interested in boys. He saw the dangers and began to remind me of my vow constantly, not just on my birthdays; those days were over. He spoke of the sacrifices he had made to enable me to live a 'normal life' in England. All he asked in return was that I keep my promise. Many single people lived happy lives, he said. Hitomi, for example, she was content with her lot.

"When I was at university, I read everything I could find about the atomic bombs and their consequences. There wasn't as much material as nowadays, but there was enough. Articles about survivors of the attack who were still suffering, who had been burned, lost their limbs, been exposed to radiation or sustained other injuries. About tumors and various diseases, cell mutations. Also about women who were pregnant when the bomb was dropped, one article in particular which I read so many times I knew it by heart. It told the story of four women who had suffered miscarriages in the wake of the bombing and four others who had managed to give birth. Some prematurely, others at full term. The authors of the article were a couple of scientists looking into the reasons why some of the women miscarried; whether, for example, it made a difference how advanced their pregnancies were, but also why two of the babies that had been born struggled with illness all their lives while the other two, both boys—or young men, at the time of writing—were healthy. Their research wasn't conclusive, not to the point where I felt reassured. They spoke about gray areas and the need for further research, about long-term effects. One of the young men had recently developed symptoms that suggested his thyroid gland wasn't functioning normally.

"And then there was this short paragraph right at the end about whether women who had been exposed to radiation were more at risk of giving birth to disabled children. They said there was no evidence of this yet, but they couldn't rule it out either. Only time would tell. 'There is still so much we don't know.'"

She falls silent. I have the impression she is getting tired. Her speech has slowed, her voice is fainter. I suggest she might want to take a rest. She shakes her head and asks if I could fetch her a glass of water.

I stand up and, in the dark, grope my way into the kitchen, guided by the glimmer of the streetlamps. I pick up a glass and fill it with water before going back to her. She cups it in both hands, raises it to her lips, takes a tentative sip as if it were a hot drink, swallows, takes another sip. Then she passes me the glass.

I place it on the table in front of us and sit down again. She clears her throat gently, continues to look straight ahead. I do the same, but this time I take her hand. She takes mine too. Her hand is cold and clammy. I try to warm it.

"The word *hibakusha* appeared in the article," she resumes. "The scientists talked about prejudice, explaining, for example, that radiation poisoning isn't contagious and debunking other myths. But I didn't feel any better. What they said about having children outweighed everything else.

"Even so I decided to tell Takahashi-san about what I had read. 'Radiation poisoning isn't contagious,' I told him. 'And there's no evidence suggesting I can't have healthy children. None whatsoever . . .'

"I knew this was only half the truth. And perhaps he sensed that. He grew increasingly sad as he listened in silence. I kept on talking, repeating the same things over and over but with less and less conviction, until at last he spoke: 'You promised me' was all he said.

"That was the same day I bumped into you in the bookshop. Do you remember?"

"Yes," I say.

"Our conversation took place that evening. When I woke the next morning, he had gone out, but he'd left a clipping from a Japanese newspaper on the kitchen table. There was a photograph of a baby cradled by its mother. One of the baby's arms was missing. One of its ears was shrunken and misshapen. Like a piece of shriveled fruit. When I deciphered the caption with the aid of a dictionary, I read that the child was also mentally disabled.

"Do you remember when he asked Naruki to come to see him?"

"Yes, but I never knew how it came about."

"Takahashi-san tracked him down," she says. "He told him that day I was a *hibakusha*. That was enough."

"Did you miss him?"

"No, because I'd just met you."

I squeeze her hand.

"Forgive me," she says, and before I have a chance to respond, she resumes: "It all happened so quickly. In my memory, at least. I remember I was heading home on the train when I got the idea . . . It was evening and the train was half empty. I was so excited I couldn't sit still. I leaped to my feet. I had found the perfect solution.

"Persuading Takahashi-san wasn't easy. But then he agreed. Of the two evils, sterilization was preferable to having to trust me to keep my promise. But he was very nervous. And so was I, of course.

"Do you remember Tokunaka-san? He was one of our regular customers. He celebrated his birthday at Nippon while you were working there . . ."

I say I remember him.

"He arranged it all. He knew a doctor who agreed to carry out the procedure."

"In Brighton?"

"Yes."

"That's why you went there that weekend . . ."

She nods.

"And you gave me your teacup before you left . . ."

"I wanted you to have something to remember me by. In case it went badly . . ."

"But it didn't," I say when she pauses. "I saw Takahashi-san the Monday after."

She doesn't reply.

"He told me you had stayed behind in Brighton . . . What happened?"

Just before we set off, the sky suddenly grew dark. We had just entered the station and stopped to look out the window at the wind sweeping the rain along the street. But then she glanced at her watch, and we continued into the building in silence, until all at once she turned to me and said: "Are you sure you want to go?"

She asked me this morning too, when I arrived at her house, and I answered then as now that I hadn't changed my mind. She seemed relieved, though I imagine that, like me, she feels a mixture of anticipation and unease.

The journey to Kure takes just under an hour. Miko warned me that the landscape between Kure and Hiroshima is rather dull: the outskirts of both cities seem to merge, and while an occasional field is visible in the distance, it's mostly industrial estates and buildings of various kinds. But she says the sea also comes into view, and that it always takes her by surprise, strange as it sounds.

She has improved greatly in the last few days and maintains

she is now less aware of the aftereffects. She has more appetite; her movements are quicker, her ripostes more playful. Occasionally I catch a glimpse of the old sparkle in her eye and her mocking smile.

Is she her "old self" again? I don't know, because the image I have of her in my mind has changed. I realized yesterday evening, when I was recalling something from our past, that I no longer see her as she was then, only as she is now. Walking through the streets of London, wearing clothes she had on earlier this week and again yesterday after I mentioned how good she looked in her jeans and blue sweater, with her hair tied up and fastened with a barrette, a red shoulder bag. This caught me by surprise, and for a moment I panicked, afraid that something terribly important was slipping through my fingers, memories dissolving, my brain failing to keep hold of them. But I gradually calmed down because I hadn't forgotten anything from the past, whether events or things we said, it was just she who had changed—or, rather, replaced herself in my mind.

I said that to her this morning. She was getting herself ready for our trip; I was sitting at the kitchen table going over in my head my ID card number, bank account numbers, names of the Icelandic presidents, the appetizers at Torg. The haiku I was going to recite to her when I got a chance. I must have been moving my lips without realizing because she asked me what I was doing. I wasn't aware she had been watching me and decided to tell her everything, about the specialist, the tests he ran, and that he seemed to suggest I might be starting to lose my faculties. I also shared my discovery of the night before, about no longer being able to see her as she was when we were young. "It came as quite a shock," I said.

"How do you see yourself?" she asked me. "When you remember the past . . ."

I had never thought about it, and now, looking back in my

mind, I realized I was nowhere to be found. "I can't see myself at all," I said. "Maybe I never have."

She leaned over me and kissed me on the forehead. "There's nothing the matter with your brain," she said. "You're the same man you were fifty years ago. The same—" She broke off mid-sentence.

"The same what?" I asked.

"All that's missing is the beard," she said, and smiled.

Naturally the train arrives on time. We sit at the back of the carriage, which is only half full. It is about eleven o'clock, still raining hard, but the wind has dropped.

The doctor's office was on the second floor of a newly constructed building in the center of Brighton. There were several other offices but none open on Saturdays. Takahashi-san handed the doctor an envelope with the money and then waited outside. She said the doctor was a man of few words, but she remembered thinking how shiny his shoes were. And how he recoiled when she told him she felt sick. She was just lying down on the treatment table and narrowly made it to the sink.

The doctor asked about the nausea. She told him it was her nerves and that she had recently started to throw up some mornings. He examined her before asking her to wait outside and motioning to Takahashi-san to come in and have a word. The doctor closed the door.

Neither of the men said anything after their conversation. She and her father left. She trembled all the way home. When they arrived, Takahashi-san confirmed her suspicions. He was frantic.

He didn't ask who the father was. But she told him anyway, in the faint hope that it might change his stance.

"Because he was so fond of you," she explained. "But it made no difference. I think he knew anyway, but he didn't acknowledge that then or later.

"He didn't blame you," she added. "He blamed me and himself."

He ordered her to stay at home but otherwise hardly spoke to her during the next few days. She became convinced she was carrying a disabled child in her belly. She lay down a lot, drifted through the house like a ghost. While he arranged everything.

When I told him I was going to my grandmother's funeral in Iceland he moved swiftly. She had no say in the matter and, in any case, wouldn't have had the strength to oppose him. He closed Nippon, booked their flights to Japan. In spite of everything, that was where his roots were.

I asked her what would have happened if I hadn't gone to Iceland. She said nothing would have changed. I had simply made their departure easier for him. She had risen from the sofa by then, had let go of my hand and was looking out the window at the quiet street and the square beyond.

She had deceived her father, committed the offense he most feared. He treated her accordingly in the months that followed.

He rented a small flat in Takehara, a village northeast of Kure. Nobody knew them there, so there was no risk of anybody recognizing her. She stayed inside most of the time, and if they went out for a stroll, it was in the evening, past the old temples and down to the harbor.

When she gave birth to a baby boy, Takahashi-san had already arranged for him to be taken immediately to a place for disabled children in Hiroshima. He couldn't believe it when the child was born healthy—with two feet, two hands, ten fingers and ten toes, the most perfectly shaped ears you could imagine, eyes that were the admiration of all. And when he cried, it sounded like the most beautiful song in the little hospital room.

It was as if the ground had given way beneath Takahashi-san's feet. Everything had been turned on its head. But he refused to acknowledge his mistake because it was too terrifying. "They'll reveal themselves later on," he kept telling her. "The defects will come out later."

The doctors knew of a couple in Kure, good people, who wanted to adopt. Takahashi-san sorted out the paperwork the day after the boy was born. She couldn't put up a fight, couldn't protest, ask to see her son again; he was gone. She had signed her name on the document. Painful as it was to relive these events, she remembered that. She had signed her name on the document.

Halfway between Hiroshima and Kure, the rain stops and the sun emerges through the clouds, which soon begin to break up. I watch the buildings fly past, old and new, factories and warehouses, shops, offices.

Before I realize it, I lean over to her and say: "Do you remember Chicken Shack?"

"What?" she asks.

"The band . . . at the blues festival in Bath . . ."

I think I see her smile behind her mask.

"Yes, what made you think of that?"

"I don't know," I say. "I've never forgotten the name."

We are looking into each other's eyes, the sun streaming through the windows, and she says: "There was nothing I could do."

She has said this before. Once when she was standing by the window, looking out at the twilight, and again yesterday, when we decided to make this trip. And I have the impression she has said it to herself many times. Countless times. For decades.

Yesterday she also said: "I was in a bad way for a long time."

She didn't explain and I didn't ask. But several years passed, two or three if my calculations are correct, before she started to study to become a teacher. And five more before she married Nakamura-san, the mathematics teacher.

It was only after Takahashi-san passed away and she got divorced that she went looking for our son. She had always known that his adoptive parents lived in Kure; the woman was Japanese and the man an Australian doctor who settled there after the war.

"They felt confident about bringing up a *hafu*," she said. "A person of mixed race. They often suffer prejudice.

"*Hafu* means half," she explained. "Half Japanese. Our son's name is Akira. He will be fifty tomorrow. He takes after you. Not just his looks."

She got into the habit of going to see him a few years ago. "What do you think he does for a living?" she asked me, and smiled.

"I don't know."

"Guess."

"A doctor?"

"He runs a restaurant. *Ramen* and *okonomiyaki*. He cooks everything himself. There are eight chairs at the bar facing the kitchen, the same number of tables in the dining room. One for six people, the rest for two or four. He's a very good chef."

She goes to see him every week. She hasn't told him who she is, and that won't change. He chats with her the same as with his other regular customers, about this and that, food, the weather; he likes jazz and football.

"He's kind," she says. "And very conscientious. I've never seen him get upset. He is good to his staff. And has a lovely smile . . . He's scared of mice."

He has two daughters, one is an engineer, the other is studying history at university. Miko has met both of them.

"The eldest is so like me when I was her age, I got quite a shock. I thought she might see herself in me. But I needn't have worried."

We plan to arrive early to be sure of getting a seat at the bar. She says he is bound to ask about me because this will be the first time she's not on her own. But she isn't worried about it and neither am I, although she hasn't discussed how she intends to respond.

As the train goes around a bend and past a small clearing, the sea suddenly appears. It really does come as a surprise, glistening and so perfectly calm that it's hard to imagine it ever being gray and storm-tossed. The sun is blazing now, and its reflections dance across the walls of the carriage.

She is gazing out at the sea. I contemplate the light on her cheek and her hair, on her neck and her slender shoulders. The last time we sat together on a train, it was on our way home from Bath. People were singing in the carriage. She was pregnant with our son.

Now she is sitting next to me, smiling at something in her thoughts. The train slows, turns shoreward. Time, distance . . . life as it might have been. She brushes her hair from her forehead and places her hand once more on the armrest between us. I need only to stretch out my fingers to touch her.